ENOCH'S PLACE

Joyce Rockwood

ENOCH'S PLACE

Holt, Rinehart and Winston / New York

All the characters in this book are fictitious,
and any resemblance to actual persons,
living or dead, is purely coincidental.

Published simultaneously in Canada by Holt, Rinehart
and Winston of Canada, Limited.
Printed in the United States of America
10 9 8 7 6 5 4 3 2 1

Library of Congress Cataloging in Publication Data
Rockwood, Joyce.   Enoch's place.
SUMMARY: Fifteen-year-old Enoch, oldest of the
children in their Blue Ridge Mountain community of
hippies, leaves his family's farm to live with his
cousins in the city.
[1. Family life—Fiction.   2. Hippies—Fiction.
3. Country Life—Fiction.   4. City and town life
—Fiction]   I. Title.   PZ7.R597En
[Fic]   79-20090   ISBN 0-03-054846-2

To my mother and father,
KAY AND BRAD ROCKWOOD

'Tis the gift to be simple
'Tis the gift to be free,
'Tis the gift to come down
Where we ought to be,
And when we find ourselves
In the place just right
'Twill be in the valley
Of love and delight.
When true simplicity is gain'd,
To bow and to bend
We shan't be asham'd,
To turn, turn will be our delight
'Til by turning, turning
We come round right.

(19th century Shaker song)

ONE

Clark's voice came up the narrow stairwell into the cold attic bedroom. A dim voice pushing into sleep. Enoch heard Mercy's name being called. Then his own came back to him in memory. His name had come first. Always the oldest was first. Without opening his eyes he pulled his face down into the warmth of the feather quilt.

Clark came a little way up the stairs. "Hey, young-uns. Morning."

"We're up," said Mercy. Already she was leaning forward on her knees to reach her clothes on the trunk at the end of her bed. Enoch could not see her through the curtain, but he could hear her when she jumped back under her quilt, dragging in her things to get dressed. Their father started back down to the kitchen. Enoch pushed the quilt away from his face.

"Clark," he said.

"Yeah?"

"I need to talk to you and Lizzie."

There was a silence, not long, but a silence.

"About going to Raleigh?" said Clark.

"Yeah."

"What's left to talk about? We said it all last night, Enoch."

"Not everything," said Enoch. "I still got things to say. Things I didn't tell you."

Silence again.

Then Clark said, "Okay. After breakfast. Now let's get the milking done."

Clark went down the stairs to the kitchen. In a moment yellow light from the kerosene lamp spilled into the stairwell and filtered up into the gray morning darkness of the attic. The back door opened and closed and the house was quiet. Outside a rooster crowed.

Enoch could hear his mother moving around in the bedroom below. Then Mercy bounced out of bed, pulled on her high-topped shoes, and clomped down the stairs with the tips of her untied shoelaces rattling lightly against the steps. Enoch heard the back door slam and her footsteps as she crossed the porch and went down the steps on her way to the outhouse. He lay staring at the ceiling, thinking about Raleigh.

Mercy returned, the back door opening and closing. He heard her pause at the wood box and then come to the foot of the stairs.

"Enoch. We need some fat lighter. You want me to get it?"

"No," he said. "I'm on my way down."

He sat up in the cold and swung his feet to the floor, his

10

long johns and wool socks holding a lingering warmth against his body. He sat slumped forward, leaning his elbows on his knees. He rubbed his hands over his face and stared down at the braided rag rug.

"Enoch. I'm going out for the fat lighter. I don't mind doing it."

"Okay, Mercy. But I'm on my way down."

He heard her go out as he stood up and pulled on his pants. He went to his wardrobe and opened the dark pine doors and took out a knit shirt and put it on. Then he reached for the flannel shirt hanging on the corner of his bookcase.

The door to the downstairs bedroom opened, and his mother walked by the foot of the stairs.

"Come on, Enoch," said Lizzie. "The cows are waiting. And it's cold down here."

"Coming." He buttoned on still another shirt, a heavy wool one, and pulled on his boots. Then he reached for his knit cap, a well-worn thing, the frazzled red yarn embedded with cow hairs and tiny chips of wood and briers and little bits of dried leaves. His cap was an old friend. His dark curly hair was shaped to fit it. If he went to Raleigh, he would take it with him.

He stepped down into the stairwell that dropped abruptly from the attic floor, making his way easily down the steep and narrow steps that wound down to the kitchen.

The kitchen was at one end of a long open room. The living room was at the other end, gray and dim in the morning dusk, barely illuminated by the lamplight from the kitchen. Lizzie was by the back door, pulling on her coat to go out.

11

"Morning," she said with a flatness in her voice that was not usual for her. She had been awake to hear what Enoch had said to Clark.

"Morning," said Enoch.

"Must be ten or fifteen degrees out," she said. "The thermometer says forty-two in here."

"Cold," he agreed, going over to the wood heater in the living room. There were coals still in it and the steel sides were warm. He lingered for a moment holding his hands against the metal. Then he opened the iron door and squatted down with the poker to rake up the coals from the ashes and judge how much kindling he would need. Closing the door with a clank, he got up to go for wood.

Lizzie was going out onto the back porch, and he waited for her to get ahead, not wanting to get embroiled yet in the Raleigh business.

"You're a regular woodsman, Miss Mercy," he heard her say as the door closed behind her.

In a moment there was a bump at the door and he opened it for Mercy, her arms full of kindling. At the top of the load was the resin-rich fat-lighter pine she had split into thin pieces with the hatchet.

"Hey, Mercy, you didn't have to do all that. I was coming." He stepped back as she came clomping in, her shoes still unlaced.

"I know," she said, dropping the wood into the box in the corner between the cookstove and the back door. "But it seems like you need help this morning." She brushed back the brown hair that had come loose from her pigtails in the night. "We do need some middle-size pieces, though. There's just big logs out there. You need to split some."

She took kindling and newspaper and went to the cookstove to make a fire in the narrow firebox.

12

Enoch went out the back door and down the porch steps and stood on the frozen earth, breathing the cold air, watching his breath pour out before him. It was good out here. Across Kettle Creek the first morning light was shining on the treetops on the crest of Brokeleg Mountain. The rest of the valley was in shadow, darkest over here against Wolf Ridge, growing faintly lighter down past the barn and across Kettle Creek.

A rooster crowed as Lizzie came out of the outhouse. Enoch watched her turn down the slope to the chickenhouse. Below, at the foot of the slope, the barn stood huge and gray, the door slightly open, the light from Clark's lamp shining out. Across the creek, on the upper slopes of the Harrimans' pasture, Enoch could see their horses grazing. And way up where he could not see, beyond the Nashes', beyond Rita's at the head of the creek, way up on the back of Wolf Ridge, he could barely hear the baying of Molly the beagle running rabbits. Ham and Soupy would be there, too, trailing along behind her.

Enoch took a log from the woodpile and reached for the splitting ax. Setting up the log, he drew back the ax and brought it up and over in an easy swing. The bit hit squarely across the end of the log and split it open in two neat pieces. He picked up one of the pieces, set it up, and split it; then the other. Then he split a second log. As he finished, he saw his mother leave the chickenhouse, eggs in both hands, and go down to the barn. He knew she was going to talk to Clark about Raleigh.

Enoch went back to the kitchen with the wood.

"Here you go," he said to Mercy. "Middle-size pieces, cut to order." With his foot he raked the kindling to the front of the woodbox and dropped his armload of wood behind it. He moved to the cookstove and warmed his hands at the fire Mercy had started. She was working now with the grain mill at the counter beside the stove. Whole wheat grains sank slowly down the hopper, and cracked wheat, for cereal, tumbled out into a pottery bowl. On the stove the blue enameled kettle made little pops and whines as it heated.

Enoch went back to the woodbox and picked out some fat lighter and some small and middle-size oak splits and went across the room to build up a fire on the pile of coals in the heater. Mercy slowed her cranking and from her lamplit place looked across at him as he knelt in the dim light of the living room.

"I don't think they want to talk any more about Raleigh," she said.

In the heater the fat lighter smoldered on the coals, pungent smoke rolling up to fill the heater and spill out of the open door into the room. Then flames leapt up and the smoke cleared. Enoch arranged the oak on the burning kindling.

"I know they don't," he said. "But I thought about it all night. One way or another, I'm going to Raleigh."

"You just *have* to go?"

Enoch did not answer. He watched the flames spread up into the oak.

"I don't want you to go," said Mercy. "I think it's a terrible idea."

Enoch shut the stove door and went around to stand close to the stovepipe, feeling for the heat.

"Have you ever been in town watching television," he said, "watching some documentary about something current and modern, and got the feeling you were a foreigner watching a show from a country that wasn't yours?"

14

Mercy stopped cracking wheat and looked at him blankly.

"It's like you were watching the BBC," he said, "or French television, or Chinese. You look at it and you think, 'That's not my world.' I feel that way sometimes. Like I was a Chinaman. But if I were a Chinaman, I could go home to Peking and flip on the TV there and say, 'Ah. That's more like it. This is what I know.' But I can't do that. I *am* home. But I feel like I'm in the wrong country sometimes. Do you know what I mean?"

"I don't think I do," said Mercy. She began turning the mill slowly. "I've never thought about anything like that."

"I didn't either when I was ten," said Enoch. "Wait about five years. You'll be glad I set a precedent."

"A what?"

"You'll be glad I paved the way for an escape from this place."

"Don't talk like that, Enoch. You make it sound like we're in jail or something. I like it here." She cranked the mill faster, looking away from him.

"I didn't mean it that way, Mercy. I like it, too. It's home. It's where I've always been. I really do like it here. I like everything about it—the house, the barn, the pasture. And you and Clark and Lizzie." It felt good to him to be speaking such things. "And I like everybody that lives around here. And I like the dogs and the cats and the horses and the cows and the chickens and the birds that sing and the salamanders in the spring and . . ."

"Okay, okay," said Mercy, laughing. "You like it. So why don't you stop talking about Raleigh?"

"I can't," said Enoch. He turned away from her, the good feeling gone. "Kettle Creek and Swallowfield—that's not all

15

there is, Mercy. I don't want to be a stranger in the world. That's all I can say. I can't explain it any other way. Let's stop talking about it." He moved away from the heater's warmth. "I'll get the sausage."

"Where's Lizzie?" asked Mercy, the brightness gone out of her voice.

"She went to the barn," said Enoch.

He went out on the back porch and took down one of the lengths of sausage that hung there from the rafters. It was fresh pork sausage stuffed in a cloth casing and frozen in the January air. He took it into the kitchen and sliced off four pieces.

"Here you go, Mercy. That big piece is for you."

She was stirring the cracked wheat into a pot of boiling water, stirring harder than was necessary, her back set firmly against him.

"You don't like the way we live, do you?" she said.

"I don't like being a hippie," Enoch said. He picked up the roll of sausage. "The cows are waiting for me," he said, and he went out.

When he was halfway to the barn, Mercy called him. He turned and saw her standing on the back steps, her arms wrapped around herself against the cold.

"Enoch, I don't *want* you to go away!"

Her voice came crisp and clear through the cold air and gave him a tightness in his chest. He waved to let her know he had heard.

They had once lived in the barn. Enoch remembered it. He could not remember before that, back when they had lived in the university town. Nor could he remember moving. But he remembered living in the barn—the awesome vastness of it, the warm smells of hay and earth and seasoned manure, the comfort of weathered planks and beams. He remembered how one end of the barn had been cluttered with building materials: lumber, dry wall, insulation, tar paper, sacks of nails. But he had no recollection of the work being done to reclaim the rundown house. Except there was one picture in his memory that must have come from that. It was Clark walking along the highest ridge of the roof, his ponytail and beard and baggy overalls silhouetted against the sky, seeming so gloriously high above the earth to his small son down below. Clark must have been shingling the roof then, but that was all Enoch remembered about fixing up the house. What he remembered most about that time was the evenings in the barn, after work was done. Even now on peaceful nights those memories would come drifting back: the circle of people around the oil drum stove, the soft lamplight, the murmur of adult voices close around him, and the music—Clark's guitar and Mountain Man's harmonica, and all their voices singing. He and Gyp Harriman would fall asleep in the midst of it, snuggled down in their sleeping bags. The two of them were the only children then. Gyp was two, Enoch four. That was back when the Callahans and the Harrimans were the only Kettle Creek families. Plus Mountain Man.

Enoch pulled back the barn door. "You want it all the way open?" he asked.

"Yeah, let's have some light in here," Clark said from the depths of the barn. As Enoch pulled the door farther back, his father stepped out from one of the stalls and set down a stainless steel milk can. The daylight, though not yet fully bright, made the lamplight inside seem dim.

17

"Frances has been asking for you," Clark said, good humor in his voice. "Your mama's milking Goldie for you."

"Thanks, Lizzie," Enoch called softly toward Goldie's stall.

"Mm-hmm," Lizzie murmured quietly, not wanting to disturb the cow.

Petunia the cat came rubbing against Enoch's ankles, and he reached down to scratch her head. She was the house cat, the pampered one. Over in the corner the half-wild barn cats were crowded around their milk pan. Everything was normal and friendly.

Enoch took the milk can and a stool and a little long-handled pan and went in to take care of Frances. To keep the milk clean, they milked with one hand, using the other to hold the long-handled pan under the teat. When the small pan was filled, they poured the milk into the tall, narrow-mouthed can, which they kept back away from the cow. It was better than milking two-handed into a bucket that the cow could kick over or shake dirt and hair into. Mountain Man had taught them one-handed milking.

As Enoch began to milk Frances, Clark came and leaned on the top rail of the stall and watched. Petunia came begging, her tail raised primly in the air, the tip of it flicking back and forth as she rubbed against Enoch's and Frances' legs.

"One shot, Tunia," said Enoch. At his voice the cat looked at him, then at the cow's udder, and seeing a teat pointed at her, readied herself, sitting back on her haunches, and caught in her mouth the stream of warm milk Enoch squirted toward her. "That's all," said Enoch, and he shooed her away with his hand.

"Now she'll spend an hour washing up," Clark said with a chuckle.

Enoch glanced at him and smiled. Everything was easy now. He almost wished the Raleigh thing would go away. There was silence except for the milk squirting into his and Lizzie's pans and the sound of the cows munching hay.

"What was it you wanted to talk about?" Clark said.

"We don't have to do it now," said Enoch.

"I think we'd better," Lizzie said from Goldie's stall. "We don't want it hanging over breakfast." She made murmuring sounds to the cow, and Enoch tried to concentrate on his own milking. Maybe he should back away from Raleigh, let it go.

But at last he said, "I just wanted to talk some more about Raleigh."

There was silence, waiting.

"Well," said Clark, "what about it?"

"When we were talking last night, I don't think I made you understand how much I want to go." His voice sounded strange to him. He did not want to say the things he was about to say.

"How much *do* you want to go?" said Lizzie.

"It wasn't that Ned came out of the blue with this invitation to come live with them," Enoch said. "I got it started. At Christmas, when they stopped to visit, I talked to Craig about it. I told him I wished I could go to that high school he goes to. I told him that things were kind of limited here in Swallowfield, and it would be nice to get out and try something new. And since we were both Callahans, our fathers were brothers and all, that it was like we were all one family, and maybe I could go live with his side of the

19

family for a while. So he said he'd talk to Ned. And I guess that's what he did. And that's why Ned and Linda wrote and asked me to come next fall."

He stopped and tried to think about how it sounded. They had never known he wanted to get away from Kettle Creek. But now they knew. He could not help it.

"What I'm trying to say is, this is not something I don't care much about one way or the other. The whole thing was my idea. I wanted it to happen. And I never thought you would say no. I never dreamed you would." His hand was growing cold and sweaty against the cow's warm flesh. He stopped and tried to dry it on his pants.

Lizzie had finished her milking. As she came out of Goldie's stall and stood beside Clark, Enoch looked up at her and felt awful. She was as she always was, thoughtful and easy. Her dark hair—Enoch's hair—curled out around her yellow knit cap. She wore her same old green jacket, faded jeans, and high-topped work shoes—like Mercy's, only her laces were tied. She was Lizzie as she always was, slender and pretty, plain with no makeup, hands rough and strong from working, but gentle hands because they were his mother's. And Clark beside her was his absolute self in his same-as-ever work pants and plaid wool shirt, goose-down vest and cap with earflaps. Enoch felt overwhelmed by their familiarity. It was painful to assault them this way. He rested his forearms on his knees and stared at his hands. He no longer felt like milking.

"You mean," said Lizzie, "you thought we'd be glad to get rid of you?"

"So long, kid, have a good life?" said Clark.

"No," said Enoch. "That's not what I mean."

20

"Well, what are you trying to say, Enoch?" Clark said impatiently.

"That I never thought you'd try to force your way of life on me, that's what. That if I wanted to try something else, you'd let me. A person has to make choices. He has to make them for himself."

He paused, still looking at his hands. Clark and Lizzie said nothing.

"You chose to live like this," said Enoch. "It was your choice. Something you decided for yourselves. But me, I was born into it. No choosing about it. Well, I have a right to make choices, too."

He went back to milking, quick and hard. Frances kicked and Enoch stopped and petted her, murmuring absently to calm her.

"What do you mean 'like this'?" said Lizzie. "What is it that's so burdensome to you?"

Enoch stopped milking again and went back to looking at his hands. He thought for a moment.

Then he said, "It's like I'm missing my time. Like I'm on the outside. The American way, whatever that is, I'm not part of it. I'm not learning it. Not like Craig is. In the summers when I go stay with him, we go zipping around in his car, going out with people, doing things. But when I'm there I always feel like a stranger, a visitor, like I'm watching but I'm not part of it. Two weeks of watching it and then I'm home again, back on the farm, working my butt off and not having anything to show for it, not any of the things he's got."

"You've got a radio," said Lizzie.

"Sure. One radio. But a car? Hah. Do you think I've got

21

any hope for that? I'll be lucky if you let me borrow the pickup truck next fall when I turn sixteen. And where would I go, anyway? To the barn dance at Tates Mill? Or maybe I could have a big night in Fairmont, go see a movie that's only two years old."

"They're not that old when they get there," said Clark. "And what makes you think I won't let you borrow the truck?"

"I don't know," said Enoch. "Nothing, I guess. But that's not the point."

"Then what is the point?" said Clark.

"The point is I'm missing out on things. Things that even y'all had growing up. You had them, so how can you deny them to me?"

"What things?" said Lizzie. "You're mystifying it."

"I can't say it any better," said Enoch. "All I can say is that the way Craig lives, that's the way everybody's growing up in this country today. That's what's on television and in magazines and newspapers. That's what the movies are about. That's the time I'm growing up in. But I'm missing it. I'm missing everything."

"Craig is the one missing out," said Clark.

"Well now, that's our opinion," Lizzie said to Clark.

"Opinion, hell," Clark said angrily. "That's truth."

For a moment they were silent. Clark looked down and began kicking slowly back and forth at a clump of straw on the floor. Enoch did not look at him directly but felt the growing pain in him and did not want it to be there.

"You don't know, Enoch," Clark said quietly. "You don't know what you're saying. You don't know how empty those things are that you want. You don't know how false they are."

"Maybe they are," Enoch said. "All I'm saying is, let me find out for myself."

Clark looked at him, but Enoch still stared down at his hands.

"Don't you think there's any way you can find out without leaving home?" Clark said. "You're not grown yet. And I like having you around. I mean, hell, you're finally old enough to carry on an intelligent conversation. I been waiting all these years."

Enoch gave a little laugh and looked up at him. Clark was smiling. But behind it was something else. A sadness. Enoch could feel it more than he could see it. He looked at Lizzie and found her looking back, thoughtful, not smiling, but not really so sad. The sadness was more with Clark.

"Those things you said last night," said Lizzie, "about a good high school with a bigger library and more courses to choose from, does all that really enter into this?"

"It enters in," said Enoch.

"Now, let's not go making decisions this very minute," Clark said to Lizzie. "Let's not get stampeded. We need to talk it over, you and me."

"That's right, Enoch," said Lizzie. "We need to talk it over. And don't go getting your hopes up, because it's definitely not settled. But we'll talk about it."

"Hey!" came Mercy's voice into the barn. "Are y'all coming to breakfast or not?"

They turned and saw her standing in the door. She was bundled up in coat and hat, her shoes tied, her mittened hands on her hips.

"The coffee's made, the cereal's done, the sausage is cooked and waiting for the eggs. Everything's ready and getting cold. So are y'all going to come or what?"

23

"Yes, ma'am, we're coming," said Lizzie, and she and Clark started for the door.

"Keep mine on the stove," Enoch called after them. "I'll be up in a minute."

"Enoch's not going to move to Raleigh, is he?" asked Mercy as she turned with Clark and Lizzie and the three of them headed up the slope toward the house.

"We don't know yet," said Clark, his voice coming faintly into the barn. Enoch could hear the sadness in it, though he tried not to.

TWO

Enoch finished milking Frances and went up to join the others at breakfast. No one was talking. When the meal was over, Clark went with Mercy out onto the porch to strain the milk and funnel it into plastic jugs, while Enoch and Lizzie did the dishes. They were still doing them when Clark came back inside.

"The milk's ready for the springhouse," he said gruffly.

"Okay," said Enoch. "Let me finish here."

"Run along," Lizzie said cheerfully. "There's not that much left. I believe I can handle it."

"Thanks," said Enoch, grateful that Lizzie did not get as wrought up about things as Clark did. He dried his hands and put on his jacket and gloves and went out onto the porch.

Mercy was waiting for him in the yard, hopping a hopscotch pattern from memory.

25

"Ready?" said Enoch as he picked up three of the jugs of milk that were on the porch table.

"Do we have to take it all?" asked Mercy, coming up the steps.

"Better had," said Enoch. "Those two we left out yesterday froze into slush before anybody came for them."

"That doesn't hurt it," said Mercy, taking the two remaining jugs from the table. She followed Enoch down into the yard.

"People don't like buying frozen milk," he said.

"They shouldn't be so finicky."

They went around the house and up the path toward the springhouse.

"Clark sure is in a bad mood," said Mercy. "What'd you say to them?"

"That I want to go to Raleigh," said Enoch. "Listen, when we get through here, why don't you run up and play with Liddle?"

"How come?" said Mercy. "What's going on?"

"They need to talk about whether or not I can go. They won't do it if we're around."

"Liddle's not home," said Mercy. "She was going up to Effie's this morning."

"Then go up to Effie's, for Pete's sake," said Enoch.

"I might," said Mercy. "But I don't know why I should help you. I don't want you to go."

"I know you don't. But you'll get used to it."

"That's what *you* say," said Mercy.

They had reached the springhouse now, and as Enoch set the milk inside, Mercy stood with her hands on her hips, mulling things over.

"I guess I'll go to Effie's then," she said at last.

"Good," said Enoch. "I appreciate it."

"I guess I'll go right now," she said. "See you later." And she started out across the hill toward the pasture.

"Are you going to ride up there?" Enoch asked.

"If I can catch Sparky, I am."

Enoch watched her climb the pasture fence, and then he turned and went back to the house. Inside he found Clark at the kitchen table sharpening the chain saw.

"Mercy's gone up to the Nashes'," Enoch told him.

"And how about you?" said Clark. "What are your plans?"

"I guess I'm going hunting," said Enoch. He walked across the room and took his rifle from the wall. From the shelf below it he picked up a box of .22 cartridges and put it in his pocket.

"Gyp going with you?" asked Clark.

"I might get him to. Or I might go alone."

"Try to get back in time to split up a little wood before dark. We need to get some ahead."

"I'll be home way before dark," said Enoch, starting out the door again.

Lizzie stepped out of the bedroom, her hairbrush in her hand.

"See you later, Enoch," she said.

"Okay," he answered. "Bye."

"Be careful," Clark said to him as he was closing the door.

"I will," said Enoch.

He crossed the porch and was on his way down the steps when an old white car pulled up the driveway. He waved to the elderly woman who was driving and took his gun back up and propped it on the porch.

27

"Who's that?" Clark called from inside.

"Luddie Belle," answered Enoch. "I'll get the milk."

He trotted down the steps and around the house and up the hill to the springhouse. When he got back with a jug of milk, Lizzie was standing by the car, her arms folded against the cold as she talked to Luddie Belle. Enoch went over and handed the milk in through the car window.

"Going hunting, are you?" said Luddie Belle.

"Thought I would," said Enoch.

Luddie Belle settled the jug of milk on the seat beside her and then picked up her purse and began looking through it for her money.

"He goes hunting most every Saturday," said Lizzie.

"Put much meat on the table?" asked Luddie Belle.

Enoch smiled. "Not much."

"He does pretty good," said Lizzie. "Squirrels and rabbits, mostly. He got us a turkey back before Christmas."

"I heard about that," said Luddie Belle, finding the two dollars and bringing them out triumphantly.

"I missed Thanksgiving by a week," said Enoch.

"The turkeys all hide before Thanksgiving," said Luddie Belle, handing the two dollars out the window. "They've been doing it ever since the Pilgrims got here."

"I guess that explains it," said Enoch.

Luddie Belle laughed. "Sure it does," she said. "That explains it, all right." She reached down and started the engine. "You ought to get yourself inside, Lizzie. It's cold out here."

"I know it is," said Lizzie.

"Thanks for my milk," said Luddie Belle, rolling up the window. Then she rolled it down again. "You be careful with that gun, Enoch."

"I will," said Enoch, and he waved as she rolled the window up again and began backing the car around.

He and Lizzie turned back to the house.

Lizzie went inside, and Enoch picked up his rifle from the porch and headed down the path toward the barn. At the June apple tree he turned off onto the path to the outhouse and made a stop there, leaving his gun on the ground outside.

Just as he was about to come out, a pickup truck came jolting up the dirt road of the valley. It was Rita's truck: by the sound alone he knew it. He listened, hoping she would slow down for their driveway. But she was picking up speed, heading on out the valley. He opened the outhouse door and looked quickly to see her, but the frost on the windows of the cab was only partly scraped away, and all he could see was the vaguest form of her inside. He came out and stood watching until the truck disappeared around the bend. Then he picked up his gun and headed down toward the barn, pushing Rita from his mind.

He began thinking of Raleigh again, wondering whether Lizzie and Clark were talking about it yet. He had a feeling they were going to let him go. When he got to the barn he stopped and looked around. This place was all he could ever remember knowing: this little valley, this house and this barn, this path that ran on to the creek. He had traveled this path so many times that he could walk it on the darkest night and never stumble and never feel afraid. If he went to Raleigh he would miss it. But that was all right. He was ready for something new.

He turned down the path again and followed it to the gate by the barn and started climbing over on the hinge side, where the gate was strongest. He stopped at the top and sat for a moment wondering whether or not to go get Gyp. Without deciding, he jumped down and headed across the pasture.

Then he came to the creek. He stopped and stood on the bank beneath the trees and watched the water flowing over the rocky streambed. The solitude of the place felt good to him, and he decided not to stop for Gyp. He would hunt alone. He would go up past Rita's house and over the back of the ridge and down across Metter Fork and up onto Skillee Mountain. You could hunt all day on Skillee and never meet a soul.

You could be lost all day on Skillee, too, like he and Gyp were that time. That was a terrible time. He was only eleven then, and Gyp was nine, and there were the two of them, wandering around lost and afraid, trying to be brave with the sun going down and night falling over them. It was awful. They had about given up hope when they stumbled onto the old mountain lady's cabin in the dark. Her dogs came running out and chased them up a holly tree, and Gyp started crying, and Enoch felt like crying but held it back because he was older and was supposed to be in charge. It took a lot to make Gyp cry. But the old lady came out and called off the dogs and helped them down from the tree. She led them inside and cooked up some hot crusty cornbread and gave it to them with plenty of butter and sorghum syrup and a big glass of buttermilk. It tasted wonderful. Then she loaded them into her old rattletrap car with her dogs in the back seat and drove them down the mountain, tearing along a twisting gravel road. Once down, she wound around the valley roads for what seemed to Enoch and Gyp a very long time, but finally she stopped at

30

the head of the dirt road that ran up the Kettle Creek valley.

"Think you fellers can find your way home from here?" she said.

"Yes, ma'am," they said and piled out, and she was gone without their knowing her name or even exactly where that cabin of hers was. It was several years before Enoch found the cabin again. It was empty then and the forest was reclaiming the clearing. She had died, he decided, because most of her stuff was still in her house. He wondered if she had had any relatives when she died, and what they had done with her dogs.

That was a couple of years ago. Enoch thought maybe he would go back up there today and see how the cabin was doing. It was an antique, if you thought about it. But nobody would ever try to save it. The roof would finally start leaking, if it had not already, and then the whole thing would rot away. That little cabin was a far cry from his uncle's brick house in Raleigh with its bay window in the living room and the soft blue carpet and the sunny yellow kitchen, immaculate and modern, and the houseplants hanging in front of the sliding glass door in the den. It would be something to live in such a fine house. No fire to start in the morning: just turn up the thermostat. No cows to milk. No chores. All your time your own. Big school. Corridors full of people. All kinds of people. Library full of books. Cars. Everywhere in cars. Anywhere. And girls. Lots of girls. A large selection. Maybe even a Rita.

The stillness of the air was broken by the sound of a tractor being cranked—a long cranking because of the cold—and then the motor started. The Harriman place

INSTRUCTIONAL MEDIA CENTER
William D. McIntyre Library
University of Wisconsin
Eau Claire, Wisconsin

stood off across the creek in the bend where the creek curved around from Wolf Ridge across the pasture. Through the bare trees, Enoch could see the tractor come chugging out of the barn, Gyp driving. It came around to the side of the barn, stopped and swung around, then backed up to a low-sided trailer that was parked there. Gyp jumped down and went back and hitched on the trailer, then climbed back in the driver's seat and took the trailer into the barn.

Enoch forgot about wanting solitude. He jumped the creek and cut up through the Harrimans' pasture to the barn—a small, rickety place, more like a combination stable and shed than anything else. Gyp was in the first stall, forking up manured straw and tossing it onto the trailer. Propping his gun against the doorway, Enoch came in and leaned against a rear tire of the tractor.

Gyp looked up with a smile.

"My very favorite job," he said, tossing a forkload of manure on the trailer. "Give me a dollar and I'll let you do it for a while."

"Thanks," said Enoch. "But I reckon I'll pass it up."

"It'd be too hard for you, anyway," said Gyp.

Enoch smiled and stood quietly, watching him work. Gyp had on old jeans, work shoes, and his denim jacket. He always wore that jacket. Under his cap his hair was fairly short—not long, anyway. He was small without being little. He was strong and quick and quietly sure of himself.

Gyp's real name was David Lamar Harriman. His mother and father had called him Davy at first, but when they moved to Kettle Creek and met Mountain Man, it got changed. "Gypsy Davy," Mountain Man would say and whip out his harmonica and play a chorus of that song, and little Gypsy Davy, only two years old, would dance and laugh and clap his hands. "He's got Gypsy hair," Mountain Man would say, "and a wandering look in his eye." It was true about the hair. It had always been dark and thick. But Enoch never did figure out where Mountain Man had gotten the notion of a wandering look. Gyp was as firmly rooted as a yeoman farmer.

Enoch watched him fork up the manure. The silence in the barn was pleasant, no strain in it.

"Going hunting?" Gyp asked.

"I don't know," said Enoch. "Started out to, but I don't know. Maybe not."

"Good day for it," said Gyp.

"Yeah, but I don't know," said Enoch. "I've got things on my mind."

Gyp forked up the soiled straw, not saying anything.

It was cold in the barn, out of the sunlight, and Enoch stuck his hands down into his jacket pockets.

"I got a letter from my Uncle Ned yesterday," he said.

"About your big plan?"

"It worked out like I wanted. He asked me to come next fall."

Gyp was silent, turning to toss straw on the trailer, turning back to fork up some more.

"I had a long talk with my folks last night," said Enoch. "They didn't go for it at all." Gyp glanced at him, smiling a little. "To tell you the truth, they surprised me," said Enoch. "They claim to be so open-minded and all. So this morning I really laid it on them."

"How's that?"

"Well, it was kind of heavy. I told them I was surprised they were being closed-minded. And I told them other

33

things. Like that I had a right to make choices. Things like that. That maybe I didn't want to be a hippie."

"Bull," muttered Gyp.

"What?"

"Just bull, that's all." He jabbed the fork angrily under some straw, turned, and threw it on the trailer. But when he turned back he was steady again. "What'd they say?" he asked.

"That they'd talk it over," said Enoch. "I guess they're talking it over right now."

"What do you think?"

"That they'll probably let me go. Lizzie was already coming around. If she can just make Clark see."

"Clark won't," said Gyp.

"How do you know?"

"I know him," said Gyp, and it was true that he did. He was more like Clark than Enoch was, more connected to the land and the seasons. Gyp spent a lot of time with Clark. He knew him.

"Well, it seems to me like he's going to give in," said Enoch. "He seems like he's resigning himself."

Gyp said nothing, but worked on in pointed silence.

"Got another fork?" Enoch said at last.

"What you can do is bring a bale of straw over here and spread it. I'm about done in this stall."

Enoch went across the barn and took a bale from the stack in the corner and brought it back to the first stall, clean now, the earth floor bare. He cut it open and began spreading the fresh straw while Gyp worked in the next stall. He wanted to tell Gyp about the good things in Raleigh. That was why he had come. But now he did not feel that he could.

"You know, I'll come home pretty often," said Enoch. "Christmas. Spring break. And then summer. All summer."

"I know," said Gyp. He stopped and turned to Enoch, leaning on the manure fork. "But you know what I think, Enoch? I think you're crazy. A goddamn fool. There's nothing in Raleigh like we got here. Nothing. You'll find out quick enough. You'll be back."

"Uh-uh," said Enoch, shaking his head. "Once I set out on this I'll stick to it. You wait and see."

"I'm waiting," said Gyp.

Enoch looked at him leaning there on the fork, staring at Enoch with his steady eyes, and with anger, a rare anger, though quiet and controlled. Enoch appreciated the anger. You, Gypsy Davy, you are my brother, he thought. But he did not say it aloud.

"Hey, come on," he said. "Let's get done with this and go hunting. Let's get a little action here."

Gyp's anger fell back, not gone but receding, no longer in his eyes but still in the set of his face. Then he smiled a little, and it was gone from that part of his face and only remained around the edges as a kind of tightness, a lack of sparkle. "Okay, my man," he said. "We'll go get us a few squirrels."

"For old times' sake," said Enoch.

"Y'ain't gone yet," said Gyp.

THREE

It seemed to Enoch that if they were going to go hunting, they ought to go ahead and go. But first they had to finish cleaning the stalls, and then they had to haul the manure to the garden, and not just dump it there, but spread it out nice and even. Then they had to take the tractor back and park it in the barn and then go up to Gyp's house to get his gun. And by that time Gyp was talking about making some sandwiches to carry along.

They reached the house and found Gyp's father standing out in the driveway talking to D. J., who was looking unusually serious.

"We're going hunting," Gyp called to Morgan. Then he added, "Hi, D. J."

D. J. lifted a hand in greeting but kept a self-conscious grimness on his face and turned back to his conversation with Morgan.

"Wonder what that's all about," Enoch murmured to Gyp as they started up the front steps.

"Don't know," said Gyp. "But I bet Daddy's not very happy about it. He wanted to write on his book all morning without any interruptions."

Enoch glanced back at D. J. and Morgan as he propped his gun on the porch. Then he followed Gyp inside.

They stopped in the living room to warm themselves at the wood stove, and they could hear Gyp's mother talking in the kitchen. Then Mountain Man said something.

"I thought he was supposed to be in Asheville today," said Gyp, turning from the stove and going into the kitchen.

Enoch followed after him.

They found Kate and Mountain Man sitting at the table, Kate winding wool onto a shuttle for her weaving, Mountain Man tilting back in his chair, one hand resting lightly on the table for balance. Mountain Man was wearing his overalls and had a stubble of beard on his face. All the gray in his whiskers made him look like an old man, though he was barely ten years older than Gyp's and Enoch's parents.

"What are you doing here, Mountain Man?" asked Gyp. "I thought this was your flea market weekend."

"It was supposed to be," said Mountain Man, rubbing his hand over his beard. "Don't I look the part?"

"What happened?" asked Enoch.

"My radiator's busted. I went out this morning to go, had my truck all loaded up, and there wasn't a drop of water in the damn thing. All leaked out."

"It must have frozen and busted," said Gyp.

"If it'd frozen, it'd still be froze," said Mountain Man. "The water wouldn't have gone nowhere. So that ain't it. It's leaking somewhere. I messed with it for an hour, but I

37

ain't found it yet. I even started out to go with it like it was. Figured I'd just stop every so often and fill her up. But I got to Swallowfield, thought I'd better check her to see how she was doing, and the thing was already half empty. Here to Swallowfield, that's one mile. So in two miles it would've been empty. A hundred miles to Asheville, that's fifty stops I would've had to make, at least. That didn't seem too reasonable, so I turned around and came back home."

"Why don't you borrow our truck?" said Gyp.

"That's what I came over here to do. But I sat down and got to talking. And then D. J. came in looking so serious about something, wanting to—quote—'have a word alone' with Morgan. Well now, I've got to wait and find out what that's about, don't I? First things first. So I've about given up on the flea market this week. Folks'll have to buy their antiques from somebody else."

"Unless they got their hearts set on buying them from a genuine mountain man," said Gyp. "Then they'll just have to wait on you."

"That's right," said Mountain Man. "If it's harmonica music and moonshine stories they want, they can wait till next week, and I'll be glad to oblige them. Anything to make them happier to part with their money. By then I'll have that cookstove fixed up. That should bring in a tidy sum." He rubbed his beard again. "I wish Morgan would hurry up with D. J. I'd like to go home and shave and get out of this mountain man suit."

"Was D. J. still out there when y'all came in?" asked Kate.

"Yeah. What's that all about?" said Gyp.

"No telling," said Mountain Man. "D. J. was right reticent about it. How about you fellers? What are you-uns up to?"

"Going hunting," said Enoch.

"Is it okay if we make us some sandwiches?" Gyp said to Kate. "Out of some of that cheese?"

"That'd be a good idea," said Kate. "Y'all are getting a late start."

"We sure are," said Enoch, following Gyp to the refrigerator to hurry him along with the sandwiches.

Gyp got out a loaf of bread and a knife.

"I hear D. J.'s got a new theory about why we call him D. J.," said Mountain Man.

"What?" said Gyp. He stopped slicing bread to listen.

"Slice," Enoch said, and Gyp went back to work.

"He thinks it's his initials backwards," said Mountain Man, laughing.

"Dubois, Jack," said Kate. "Very good. Only thing is, he's wrong."

"He'll never figure it out," said Gyp, handing the slices of bread to Enoch, who was ready with the mayonnaise. Gyp started slicing the cheese.

They heard the front door open, and Kate leaned back in her chair and craned her neck to look into the living room. It was Morgan.

"Where's D. J.?" Kate asked him.

"Gone home," said Morgan. "I lent the son of a bitch thirty-five dollars. We may as well kiss it good-by."

"You did what?" said Kate, straightening around in her chair as Morgan came into the kitchen.

"Well, I did it for Wanda, really," said Morgan. "She's pregnant, and they don't have the money for her to go to a doctor about it."

"Pregnant?" said Mountain Man, bringing his chair down on all four legs.

"Of all the dumb things," said Kate. "What are they

going to do? Don't tell me D. J.'s going to get out and get a job?"

"Lord, no," said Morgan. "Not while he can still draw unemployment."

"We don't call him Drawing Jack for nothing," said Mountain Man.

Kate smiled. "Mountain Man says D. J.'s got a new theory about his nickname."

Enoch and Gyp had their sandwiches wrapped and were stuffing them into their jacket pockets.

"We've heard this already," said Gyp. "We'll see y'all later."

"Don't shoot each other," said Mountain Man.

"We'll try not to," said Enoch as they went out of the kitchen.

"When will y'all be home?" Morgan called after them.

"Soon," Enoch answered. "I've got to split wood this afternoon."

"Okay then. Good luck," said Morgan.

"Thanks," they both said.

Gyp went to the closet in the hallway and got out his .22 rifle. Then he followed Enoch outside.

It was midafternoon when Enoch and Gyp came down from Wolf Ridge and split up at the ford in Kettle Creek. Enoch hurried across the pasture, still thinking of Raleigh, anxious to get home and learn what Clark and Lizzie had decided. He climbed over the gate, and as he came around the barn and started up the hill, he saw Bud and Betty's van parked in the driveway. He wondered if it was Bud or Betty. It could be both if Gladys was minding the store in Swallowfield. And since this was Saturday, she probably was. Gladys was only Gyp's age, but already people were saying that it was her natural calling to run her parents' bakery and health food café.

As Enoch came up the slope by the chickenhouse, the outhouse door opened and Mountain Man came out. When he saw Enoch he stopped by the June apple tree and waited for him. Mountain Man looked different now. He was clean-shaven and was wearing jeans and a plaid flannel shirt under an open parka.

"Any luck?" he asked as Enoch approached.

"Nah," said Enoch.

"Not even a near miss?"

"I reckon we weren't trying all that hard," said Enoch. "We saw a squirrel or two, but we didn't take a shot."

"Not hungry enough," said Mountain Man.

Enoch smiled. "I guess not," he said.

"It was different when I was a boy," said Mountain Man. "Seems like we were always meat hungry. It changes the way you hunt. Makes it real serious. I reckon it's better your way."

They trudged up the steps onto the porch.

"I think I could hunt to live, if I had to," said Enoch.

Mountain Man pushed open the back door.

"You probably could," he said, and the two of them went into the kitchen.

Bud and Betty were sitting at the kitchen table drinking coffee with Clark and Lizzie. Betty had been talking, but she paused when Mountain Man and Enoch came in.

"Y'all are missing a good story," Clark said.

"Yeah, you got to hear this one, Mountain Man," said Bud. "Old Gladys pulled D. J. out of the fire yesterday. Start over, Betty."

"You can just summarize," said Mountain Man, taking his half-empty mug from the table and going over to the coffeepot on the stove. "Coffee?" he said to Enoch, who was putting away his rifle.

"Yeah, thanks," said Enoch.

"Well, to summarize," said Betty, "Gladys was minding the store yesterday, selling a cake to Thelma Collins, of all people, when in floats D. J., doped up on God knows what."

Mountain Man returned to the table with two steaming mugs and shoved one toward Enoch, who was pulling up a chair.

"Did Thelma notice?" asked Mountain Man.

"Not until D. J. grabbed her arm and told her the starship was landing in thirty minutes and she better run home and get her bags packed."

"God amighty," said Mountain Man, slumping down in his chair. But then he could not help laughing. None of them could.

"He was really out of his mind," said Betty. "Gladys said that at first she was going to try to cover for him, because of Thelma, but when D. J. said that about a starship, Gladys gave up trying to pretend he was normal."

"What'd old Thelma do?" asked Mountain Man.

"Actually, she was rather heroic," said Betty. "It scared her but she didn't want to run out and leave Gladys alone with D.J."

"Those old ladies have more spunk than we give them credit for," said Bud.

"But now Gladys has to handle both of them," said Betty, "because here comes Thelma behind the counter to stand by her, and Gladys sees her eyes sweeping around like she's looking for a weapon."

42

"Oh, god," said Lizzie.

"But Gladys stays cool," said Betty. "She throws a towel over a knife that's lying there and starts trying to calm Thelma down. 'D. J.'s not dangerous, Miz Collins,' she says. 'He's just drunk is all.'

"Well, Thelma's no fool. She says, 'He seems more than drunk to me. Seems like he's on some kind of dope.'

" 'Oh, no,' says Gladys. 'He always gets like this when he's drunk.'

"Now, meanwhile, D. J.'s ordering a cheese and sprout sandwich on whole wheat with extra mayo and sounding so straight about it that Thelma starts relaxing. Gladys tries to give her the cake and send her on her way. But then all of a sudden D. J. starts begging Gladys not to go with the starship. And that does it. Gladys lets him have it. She says, 'You get out of here, Jack Dubois. I'm not fixing you any kind of sandwich. You go home and sleep it off.'

"Then Thelma chimes in. 'That's right, young feller,' she says. 'You take your business elsewhere or we'll be calling the sheriff to you.'

"But now D. J. puts his head down on the counter, and he starts crying. He doesn't want Gladys to go with the starship. So Gladys gives up. She picks up Thelma's cake and takes Thelma by the elbow, and out they go through the front door.

"Of course, the first thing Thelma wants to do when she gets outside is go call Tommy Tate. 'That boy ought to be locked up,' she keeps saying. But Gladys talks her out of it. She tells her D. J. is just drunk and she'll go upstairs and get her daddy to drive him home."

"Of course, I was off at the wholesaler's in Fairmont," said Bud. "But Thelma didn't know that, so she went on

43

home, and Gladys went upstairs and got Betty."

"When she told me about it," said Betty, "I could've killed D. J. I sent her across the road to get Donovan while I went down and sat with D. J. Donovan came and took him home. I don't know what he was on. His pupils were as big as dinner plates."

"Gladys should've let Thelma call the sheriff," said Bud. "I'd like to see Drawing Jack run right out of the county."

"I wouldn't," said Enoch.

"Why not?" said Betty. "He makes us all look bad, carrying on like that."

"But I feel sorry for him," said Enoch. "You can tell he wants to get straightened out. He just can't somehow."

"He's losing ground, if you ask me," said Clark. "Got fired at the sawmill for smoking pot on the job. Drawing unemployment now for six months, not stirring to find another job. Not putting in a crop. Not hiring out as a hand. Not nothing. Just drawing and getting wasted on dope and listening to that damn stereo."

"And knocking Wanda up," said Betty.

"Yeah," said Bud. "What kind of future is that poor kid going to have?"

"Wanda or the baby?" said Lizzie.

"Both," said Bud.

"See?" said Enoch. "That's why we ought to cover for him. At least here he's got a chance of coming around."

"I think he's hopeless," said Betty.

"Nobody's hopeless," said Enoch.

"Some people are," said Mountain Man. "Maybe not D. J., but I've known hopeless people. Met them when I was living in Asheville mostly, usually in bars. I mean folks that there ain't nothing going to bring them around. But then I also met some that seemed hopeless and turned out not to be."

"What about D. J.?" said Enoch.

"I don't know," said Mountain Man. "The odds are against him, I reckon."

"Hey, Enoch," said Betty, her voice bright to break the mood. "Reach us that coffeepot behind you."

Enoch got up and took the pot from the stove and poured another round. He sat down again, and there were a few moments of passing cream and honey and stirring coffee.

Then Mountain Man said, "So you want to try city life, do you, Enoch? You don't think it would be any good for D. J., but you want it for yourself."

"I'm not a dopehead like he is," said Enoch. "I can handle it." He glanced at Clark and Lizzie.

"I'll tell you what we've decided," said Lizzie. "We're going to pass the buck. We're leaving it up to you. If you want to go, you can go. But only on the condition that you don't make up your mind until summer. You take time until then to think it through."

"All the way through," said Clark.

Enoch grinned, raising his arms triumphantly.

"Whoa!" warned Clark. "No celebrations. You've not decided yet, don't forget."

"How can I keep from deciding?" said Enoch. "Do you want me to pretend my mind's not made up?"

"Yeah," said Clark. "That would do for a start."

"The thing is," said Mountain Man, "you don't announce any decision until summer. That makes changing your mind a little easier. You just wait. You might be glad to have an out."

"If you want to know about life in the suburbs," said

45

Betty, "come talk to me about it some day. I had eighteen years of it. I'm an expert."

"I had twenty," said Lizzie.

"I was lucky," said Clark. "Morton was so small we didn't have suburbs."

"There wasn't any kind of town at all where I grew up," said Mountain Man. "Just me and Mama and Daddy and my two sisters and the hogs and the chickens up yonder on Jenkins Ridge. Unless you want to count that time I spent in Cincinnati. But that wasn't suburbs. That was inner city. Whoo!" He shook his head.

"I never can imagine you in Cincinnati," said Lizzie.

"I don't remember hardly a thing about it myself," said Mountain Man. "Just that big school where I went to first and second grade. And the front stoop on that place where we lived. Funny I don't remember the inside. But what I remember most about Cincinnati is that night they got Daddy. Seems like that blocks out all the rest. To my dying day I'll never forget them company goons sprawling me across the sidewalk while they busted my daddy's kneecaps. I never will forget the way he sounded, lying there groaning while they went running off into the night. I got up, but he couldn't. He never did walk again."

"Just because he was for the union," said Enoch.

"He wasn't just in favor of it," said Mountain Man. "He was organizing for it. He was a good organizer, too. That's why they got him. And that put an end to our little sojourn in Cincinnati. We came back home to Jenkins Ridge, and that's where I remember growing up."

"But you've lived in suburbs," said Clark. "When you were in Asheville."

"Oh, hell, I don't even want to think about that," said

Mountain Man. "That tacky little brick house in a damn ocean of brick houses. Wasn't any difference between any of them except the color of the shutters. And me working two jobs to pay the mortgage on the thing. And Mary running around on me because I never was home. Fifteen lost years. She did me a favor when she divorced me. It hurt, her taking the two boys away, but she did me a favor. I quit both my jobs the next day and got out of there. Came back home. Don't ask me about suburbs, Enoch. I've got intentional amnesia."

"Then ask me," said Bud. "I came up in the belly of the monster. Southern California. God, it was awful. I couldn't get out of there fast enough."

"Well, it couldn't have been that bad for all of y'all," said Enoch. "Y'all turned out all right."

Mountain Man laughed and slapped the table.

"It was the times that saved us," said Lizzie. "The sixties."

"But there's more to it than that," said Mountain Man, sitting back in his chair with his mug of coffee. "There's who done the raising. You-uns had folks that struck a spark of thoughtfulness in you, and a spark of decency to go with it. They might not have fanned the flames, but they struck the sparks." He laughed softly. "My old daddy started a fire in me and fed it kerosene. It just took me a while to feel it."

He was thoughtful now, and the others sat quietly, knowing there was more.

"Funny, it's Raleigh you should be aiming to run off to, Enoch," he said. "One of my boys is there."

"In Raleigh?" said Lizzie. "I thought they were living in Charlotte now."

"Not Ralph," said Mountain Man. "He came to see me

47

last spring and told me he'd be taking a job in Raleigh soon as he graduated."

"Ralph came here?" said Clark. "You didn't tell us that."

"No," Mountain Man said quietly, "I didn't." He was leaning back in his chair, holding his coffee mug with both hands, as if to warm them. "He came with two college buddies. They drove up in a red Pontiac. One of them sporty jobs, you know. I don't know what you call it—F-16, Spitfire, some airplane sounding name. The inside of the damn thing was white. Pure white, I tell you."

"Whose car was it?" asked Lizzie.

Mountain Man knew what she was thinking.

"Yeah," he said. "I was hoping it wasn't Ralph's, too, but turned out it was. That's my boy's idea of transportation. Seems pretty far gone, already, don't he? But that ain't the half of it."

"He's young," said Bud. "Kids get into things like that. How old is he now? Twenty?"

"Twenty-two," said Mountain Man. "And like I said, that ain't the half of it. They drive up and out they pile, the three of them, dead drunk. Now I don't mind folks drinking if they don't act drunk. But when these idiots piled out and started staggering around and giggling, I near about walked off and left them. But I thought better of it. After all, this was the first time I'd had one of my boys come to see me. I figured I'd better stick it out. So I took them in and put some coffee down them and got them straightened up a little. Learned they were on their way to Gatlinburg. One of the other boys' folks had a vacation house over there, and they were on their way to whoop it up and have a wild weekend. Said they were going to pick up some local girls."

"That's what they all say," said Betty.

48

"Well, Ralph could if anybody could," said Mountain Man. "He's a handsome dude. I got to give him credit for that. But it ain't my kind of handsome. Too slick looking. He must work on it day and night. It'd been four years since I'd seen him last, but he still looked the same as I remembered—like he'd just walked off a mouthwash commercial."

"Looks aren't everything," said Enoch. "Inside he might be different."

Mountain Man shook his head. "They sat there in my house drinking their coffee and feeling uncomfortable. I got the feeling Ralph hadn't wanted to come. See, he'd made the mistake of telling them he had a daddy in the nieghborhood. So the other two got all hot on having a reunion. Ralph didn't know my exact circumstances, but he did know I wouldn't be living in no brick house. I don't think he was prepared for the cabin, though, and the chickens and the pig and the junk in the yard. I tried to tell him it was future antiques, but he was embarrassed, I could tell.

"So we talked about his school. He was about to graduate, you know. He said he was majoring in business. Well now, I thought, that's not so bad. A feller with a good business head could run a hardware store, and that's not so bad a life. So I asked him what line of business he's planning to go into, and he said real estate. I thought, great god amighty, he's going to be selling brick houses to poor sons of bitches that'll have to take two jobs to pay for them and put their wives to working, too. I didn't feel like I could just nod pleasantly and say that was nice. So I told him about that trip I took with Bud and Betty to California a few years back, and how we drove through Arizona and saw those land development schemes in the middle of the damn desert. You remember those?"

49

Bud and Betty nodded.

"They had streets all laid out in neat gridirons," said Mountain Man, "and street signs on the corners, like in a regular town. But that was all there was. Nothing else but tumbleweeds and cactus. I mean nothing. Just streets laid out in the middle of the desert and a big sign saying 'Welcome to Sun City'—or some such thing."

"There were a few houses," said Betty.

"I'm coming to that. But first I want you to get the picture of nothingness. The houses don't change that. There were just three or four of them scattered here and yon in the distance, not even near the highway, but each on its own little lot on its proper street in that great wide emptiness. They were old folks, you can bet on it. Got talked into spending their life savings on a retirement home in sunny Arizona. And there they were, miles from everything, from grocery stores and doctors and their families back east, stuck out there in the middle of the desert in a damn brick house."

Clark whistled under his breath and shook his head. The others were silent, waiting for Mountain Man to go on. But he just stared at the table.

"What'd Ralph say to that?" Betty asked at last.

"He said that was real estate at its best—to take a piece of worthless land and make it somebody's life dream."

"I can't believe it," said Lizzie.

"He said he wanted to get into mountain developments, but he was going to start out selling for subdivisions in Raleigh. The father of one of his buddies had a business and was going to take him on."

"Probably the guy with the house in Gatlinburg," said Bud.

"I reckon," said Mountain Man. "I felt too bad to ask. I was thinking about my daddy and all he gave me, and here was my boy standing before me and I hadn't given him one damn thing. Nothing. I had him for ten years. I could've given him something. But I was too busy working, too busy trying to give him a brick house and a Chevrolet and a TV and shiny toys. So Mary and her feller took him and made him a real estate developer. I don't feel like he's mine. Enoch there is more mine than Ralph is."

Enoch met his eyes and smiled a little.

"But Enoch doesn't know what he's gotten from you," Clark said sullenly. He was staring at his cup, moving it slowly back and forth on the table.

"I do, too," said Enoch. "You've given me a whole lot, Mountain Man."

"Well, don't think that's going to keep him from leaving," Clark said, looking up in anger. "He's obviously made up his mind to go, and to hell with all of us."

"Now, Clark," said Betty, laying a hand on his arm.

"Yeah, Clark," said Lizzie. "Take it easy."

"But isn't it true?" said Clark, his voice rising as he got to his feet. He glared at Enoch. "Do you really care? Do you care what we've given you? Hell, no!"

Clark turned and strode out of the house, slamming the door behind him.

Enoch stared for a moment at the door. Then he slammed down his coffee mug and pushed back his chair and stomped up the stairs to his room.

FOUR

Appalachian winters taper off in February. Clumps of green daffodil leaves poke out of the ground, testing the air. Tree buds swell perceptibly, then stop and wait. Except the willow does not wait. It comes ahead with tiny leaves, yellow in their infancy, hardy against the freezes still to come. As the month passes, cold days are broken up by warmer ones. Farmers walk their fields and tinker with their tractor motors. Spirits lift and people grow more sociable.

In a vase in the window of the little kids' room in the schoolhouse was a sprig of apple blossoms brought to premature bloom by the warm indoors. Enoch sat on the rug in the audience—big, middle, and little kids together—and looked beyond the blossoms at the rain.

"Announcing," said Mary Lou, standing up in front,

" 'The Mystery of Skillee Mountain,' a one-act play written and directed by Mary Lou McCall and Billy Boy Nash."

"Starring," said Billy Boy, who was standing beside her, "Billy Boy Nash and Mary Lou McCall. And co-starring Roland and Robbie Nash."

"You mean Dee and Dum," Effie said from the audience.

Billy Boy smiled out at his older sister. Then he took a sidelong glance at his mother. Melinda looked back at him sternly.

"I'd better not," Billy Boy stage-whispered to Effie. "Co-starring," he repeated, "Roland and Robbie Nash." But then, glancing again at his mother, he added quickly, "Also known as Tweedledee and Tweedledum."

Melinda pursed her lips as the little twins popped their heads above the front table and waved to the cheering audience. Enoch laughed and settled back for the upcoming production. He saw that Bill Nash—father of the young Nashes and teacher, with Melinda, of the Kettle Creek School—was laughing, too.

Enoch and Mercy walked home from school with the rain still falling in a mist. The dirt road down the valley was muddy, and they picked their way along the high places. They found the house silent. Clark was off somewhere—the truck was gone. Lizzie was not home yet from substitute teaching at the high school in Fairmont. They went inside and for a little while the radio blared as they added wood to the heater and fixed snacks for themselves. Then all became quiet again. Mercy was upstairs reading. Enoch was reading at the kitchen table, tilting his book to catch the light of the kerosene lamp. His concentration was total.

Then Soupy trotted off the back porch—Enoch heard her

toenails as she scrambled to her feet and went down the steps. In a few moments the truck pulled into the driveway. Then there was stomping and foot-scraping on the steps as Clark worked to get the mud off his boots. Finally the back door opened. Clark came in, looking down behind him saying, "No, Soupy, you have to stay out," and shutting the door gently in the dog's face.

"Hi," said Enoch, closing his book but keeping his finger in his place.

"How's it going?" said Clark.

"Pretty good. Is it still raining?"

"No, it's starting to clear off. Looks like it'll be nice for a while. Feels kind of warm."

"Mountain Man had some daffodil buds in his yard today," said Enoch. "But they'll just be those ugly raggedy ones. You know, the ones that are kind of green? They always come first."

"Yeah, they are ugly," said Clark. He took the coffeepot to the sink and ran water in it. "Where's Mercy?"

"Upstairs."

"Hiya, Mercy!" Clark called.

"Hi, Clark," she called back, but nothing more. No move to come downstairs.

"She's reading," said Enoch. "Nancy Drew, I think. Fine literature."

"That's all right," said Clark. "If it's fun for her. How was school today?"

"Good," said Enoch. "Got a new book." He held up the paperback he had been reading.

"Hey, *The Frontiersmen*," said Clark. "I've been hearing about that for years. Never could find a copy." He took the book from Enoch, losing his place.

"Melinda special-ordered them in Fairmont," said

54

Enoch. "Gyp and Gladys got one, too. It's really something. It's like a novel, but it's real. In the back there's notes for each chapter, showing the research that he did and all. It's about Kentucky and Ohio and up in there, but Melinda says it's not that different from what happened around here. Down here it was Cherokees that had the land. Up there it was Shawnees."

Clark turned to the back of the book and whistled under his breath. "Seven hundred pages."

"Yeah, but it's good. I've already read sixty pages of it."

"I'd like to read it when you're done," said Clark, giving the book back to him. "What else at school today?"

"Not much. Same old stuff mostly. Except Mary Lou and Billy Boy did a one-act play they had written. One scene was all it was, really. But it was funny."

"Eight-year-old playwrights?" said Clark.

"Yeah, and not bad ones. What was really hilarious was that Billy Boy had written in parts for Dee and Dum. They were supposed to play puppies. You wouldn't think three-year-olds could understand about a play. But there they were, crawling around all over the place and barking. We about died laughing." Enoch chuckled.

"Those two'll do anything for Billy Boy," said Clark, and he moved the boiling coffee to a cooler part of the stove. "Say, Enoch," he said. "Think you could tear yourself away from that book for a while?"

"What do you need?"

"I was in the post office a while ago," said Clark, "and I mentioned to Hub that Luddie Belle didn't come by for her milk yesterday. He said he'd heard she was sick. Didn't know what with. Old age, I reckon. Whatever it is, she'd probably appreciate having her milk delivered."

"Can I take the truck?" said Enoch.

"You know you can't."

"One of these days I'm going to ask you that and you're going to forget and say yes."

"That'll be the day you turn sixteen and get your license," said Clark.

"I'll be—" Enoch stopped short, thinking better of saying he would be in Raleigh when that happened.

But Clark had caught it. He smiled a little. "You don't know what you'll be," he said, pouring himself a cup of coffee. He picked up the newspaper that was on the table and went to the sofa on the other side of the room.

"I'll be glad when I'm sixteen and you let me drive alone," said Enoch, trying to smooth it over.

"Me too," said Clark. But the light had gone gray between them.

Enoch got up and put out the lamp. "I'll be back in a little bit," he said. "Do you need anything from town?"

"Not that I can think of," said Clark, disappearing behind the newspaper.

Upstairs Mercy bounced from her bed.

"Wait, Enoch," she called and clattered down the steps, jumping the last two into the kitchen. "I want to go."

"Get your jacket," he said.

She grabbed it from the back of a kitchen chair and started after him. But he stopped and looked back toward the stairwell doorway.

"Mercy," he said, "did you leave your lamp on?"

"Oh, gosh," she said and turned back.

"Mercy," Clark said sternly, lowering his newspaper to look at her.

"I'm sorry, Daddy. I just forgot." Then she stopped still, staring in horror at the stairwell.

Petunia the cat came trotting down into the kitchen.

"Oh, Mercy," said Enoch. "Not the cat, too."

She looked from Enoch to Clark, her eyes wide.

"Mercy!" Clark said sharply. "Come here."

Mercy walked stiffly over and stood before him.

"What have we told you about that?"

"That it's dangerous," she said softly.

"What is?" said Clark.

"To go out and leave the lamp burning. Especially if Petunia or Soupy are inside because they can knock it over."

"Then why did you do it?"

"Because I was in too much of a hurry," she whispered, looking down. "I'm sorry."

"It's the second time," said Clark. "You should be punished. Perhaps we should let Enoch go to town alone."

"Oh, Clark," she said, and tears came to her eyes.

"Or maybe you should do some extra milking," said Clark.

"Milking. I'll do Mama's share tonight."

"Okay," said Clark. "But don't dawdle too long in town. Run up now and blow out the lamp."

She turned and ran for the stairs. Glancing up at Enoch, she found his face no longer stern but gentle in support.

In a moment she was back again, and by the time they were down the porch steps her bounce had returned.

"Let's ride," she said.

"I'd rather walk."

"Oh, come on, Enoch. You never ride anymore. Reno will go wild if you don't ride him."

"I thought Gyp had been riding him some."

"He has," she admitted. "But come on anyway. Let's ride. Please?"

Enoch gave in. They took the path to the pasture, stopping at the barn to get bridles and a bucket with some feed. The horses were on the far side of the pasture near some trees on the lower slopes of the ridge. Mercy called them and clanged the bucket and waved it to show them she had feed for them. The horses only stood and looked. Enoch and Mercy had to walk all the way to them.

"There was this English dude that came over to visit America in colonial times," Enoch said as they trudged up the ridge. "He wrote home that Americans will walk two miles to catch a horse to ride one mile."

"This isn't two miles," said Mercy.

"Yeah, but the principle's the same."

The four horses finally stirred themselves and came the last ten yards to meet them. After Mercy gave a taste of feed to all four, she and Enoch bridled Reno and Sparky. Enoch gave Mercy a leg up on Sparky, then led Reno to a stump. It was too low to make a good mounting block, and he had to struggle to pull himself high enough on the horse's bare back to get a leg over.

"Hey, there's Liddle," said Mercy as Enoch straightened himself. He looked where she was pointing—down across the slope to Kettle Creek. From horseback they could see farther up the creek than before, and there, sure enough, was Gyp's sister. Alone beneath the bare trees, she was practicing ballet, using a broken sapling for a bar.

"I can do that," said Mercy. "It's the new thing Geneen taught us yesterday." She sat quietly, watching Liddle move gracefully through the exercise. "But Liddle can do it better," she said at last.

"She practices," said Enoch.

"So do I," said Mercy. "But Liddle does it better from the start."

It was also true that Liddle practiced. Enoch had often seen her. He would catch sight of her there by the creek, or up on the ridge, or in the dim shadows of the barn. He knew what it was with her. Away from the other children she acted out her daydreams, pretending to be a renowned dancer or guitar player or singer, for she excelled in all those things and worked at them.

"I'm going to go see if she wants to come with us," said Mercy.

"Nah, leave her alone," said Enoch. "She's having fun."

"Practicing ballet?" said Mercy, looking at him incredulously.

Enoch shrugged. "Do what you want," he said. "I'll meet you down on the road. I've got to stop back by the springhouse for the milk."

He thought he would have to wait for them on the road, but they came along at a gallop, the two of them holding themselves easily to Sparky's bare back. They reached the meeting place when Enoch did.

"Here you go again, Liddle," said Enoch. "Letting Mercy stop you from practicing."

"I know it," Liddle said, almost regretfully. "But I was tired, and . . . I don't know. Sometimes I want to practice, other times I want to do things with people. Anyway, I've been practicing since I got home from school."

"That's pretty good," said Enoch. "Let's get going, or we'll be coming home in the dark."

They started down the dirt road, Mercy and Liddle going ahead on Sparky, Enoch coming behind with the jug of milk. Near the end of the road they passed D. J. and Wanda's place and then turned right onto the grassy shoulder of the paved road. They were in Sugar Valley now.

There were six farms on the flat, fertile land. Five belonged to people with longtime roots in the area. The sixth farm belonged to Brandy and Stuart McCall.

The milk expedition broke up at the McCalls' farm. Brandy was outside with Mary Lou and Janie. They all waved, and Liddle could not pass them by. Liddle had a special attachment for Brandy because Brandy was a musician, too. Once she had been a violinist and had played in orchestras, but she had given it up to get away from cities. Now she taught music in the Kettle Creek school and went to Fairmont once a week to give private lessons. More than anyone else, Brandy understood Liddle's dreams and nurtured her talents. Liddle liked being around her.

"Let's stop here," she said to Mercy.

"No, let's go with Enoch."

"I'm staying here," said Liddle, and she slid down from Sparky's back.

"Oh, all right," Mercy said, turning the horse into the driveway.

"Don't stay long," said Enoch. "You've got all the milking to do, don't forget."

Mercy made a face.

"*All* the milking?" Liddle said as Enoch rode away.

"Left on the crazy old lamp," Mercy said, and after that Enoch could not hear them anymore.

The valley farms stopped at Sugar Creek. The road crossed the creek on a concrete bridge and then came to an end at the state highway. The junction of the two roads formed the heart of Swallowfield. There was no traffic light in the town, just a stop sign or two. Nor was there much in the way of commerce. There were McPhee's General Store and the post office side by side in one building. Enoch could remember when Gyp's grandparents ran the store—back before they sold out to Bert McPhee. Next to the store was a little space of yard shaded by an old hickory tree, and next to that was Bud and Betty's Baked Goods and Food for Wholesome Living: B&B's most people called it. Enoch saw Bubba at the foot of the stairs beside B&B's.

"Bubba," he called and waved.

The little boy turned his face away with a smile and headed up the stairs. The Stroupes—Bud and Betty, Gladys and Bubba—lived above their store.

The next building down from B&B's was an old boarding house that had long ago been converted to apartments. Mostly old people lived there. Across the road, between Sugar Creek and the highway, was Donovan and Geneen's craft store and, next to that, Rudy Roger's garage and gas station. The only other commercial establishment in Swallowfield was Neese's Grocery and Gas on the far edge of town toward Fairmont. There were two churches in town, Baptist and Holiness, and two cemeteries, one in the yard of the Holiness Church, the other, nondenominational, on a slope above the town.

Most of the houses in Swallowfield were old but neatly painted. Yards were large enough to have vegetable gardens in them. Some people had chickens. Many of the gardens were terraced because of the steepness of the land. The streets running back from the highway went uphill and connected with a street that ran parallel to the highway. It was called Backstreet, though according to the records in the city office in the back of McPhee's Store it was Wilson Avenue. From Backstreet a few gravel roads ran steeply up the slopes to small, poor houses perched on the hillside. Luddie Belle's house was one of these.

61

Enoch rode up the hill, dismounted, and tied Reno to the bumper of Luddie Belle's aging car. He took the milk to the front door and knocked. There was no response. He peered in through the lacy curtains that covered the windows in the top half of the door and could see the silver-gray light from the television. He knocked louder and then saw movement within the front room. He stopped looking and waited. In a few moments Luddie Belle opened the door.

"Why, Enoch Callahan! You dear thing. Brought me my jug of milk."

"Well, I was coming to town," he said. "I thought you might like to have it brought up."

"Bless you for thinking of me, Enoch. Bless you, bless you. Now, don't you run off. Come on in and give an old lady some company."

"I reckon I'd better be getting on back, Miz Luddie."

"Nonsense," said Luddie Belle, opening the door further. "Come in and have some pie. That's an order, young feller."

"Well, if it's an order," said Enoch, smiling, and he stepped inside. "What kind of pie?"

Luddie Belle laughed. "I knew the pie'd get you."

Enoch followed her through the cluttered living room to the kitchen. She looked in the refrigerator, moved around a few things, and pulled out a pie pan covered with a plate. She lifted the plate curiously.

"Lemon!" she exclaimed. "One piece left. Just enough."

Enoch saw it was a quarter of the pie. Even without Lizzie there to remind him, he knew he did not want that much sweet stuff in one sitting.

"I'll take half of that," he said. "You take the other half."

"No, no. It's all for you," she said and set the pie pan in

front of him. "You don't mind eating from the pan, do you? Hold on now, and I'll get you a fork. And a glass of milk. I've got good fresh milk, you know. Just delivered."

"Really, Miz Luddie. I can't eat this much. You take part of it."

Luddie Belle wrinkled her nose and shook her head. "I don't much care for pie," she said. "Too sweet."

Enoch laughed. "Then who ate the rest of it?"

"Preacher Martin. And Mattie Fitzgerald next door. Now where is that purse of mine? I got to give you some money for the milk." She searched the kitchen counters, then disappeared into her bedroom. Immediately she reappeared. "The fork," she said. "I forgot it." She came back and got a fork from a drawer and then produced a glass for his milk.

"I'll pour it," said Enoch.

"All right, you pour it. I'll go look for—whát was I looking for? Oh, yes, my purse." She disappeared again.

In a moment she returned. "Two dollars for the milk," she said, "and a little extra for bringing it." Enoch reached out and took the two dollars but pushed back the fifty cents she offered. "The pie is for delivery," he said. He took another bite and smiled.

"Ah, well. Have it your way." She sat down at the table with him. "Did they tell you I was feeling poorly?"

"Hub Iverson told Daddy."

"I don't know what it is. I get so tired sometimes. Don't feel like I can get up my strength to get out. It's old age, I reckon. You just can't live eighty-six years without running down toward the end. But you wouldn't know how it is, would you, Enoch? When you're young, you can't imagine getting old."

"Well, I've always heard it's better to be old than to be

63

dead," said Enoch, glancing at her playfully.

Luddie Belle laughed and reached out and grabbed his arm. "It *is*," she said, squeezing his arm and shaking it. "It is."

"I think it was you who told me that," said Enoch and took another bite of pie.

Luddie Belle smiled and settled back in her chair. "Where's that Miss Mercy?" she said.

"I just left her off at the McCalls'," said Enoch. "Her and Liddle."

"They didn't want to come see me, huh?"

"They did, but they got sidetracked."

"You tell them about the pie they missed."

"I will," said Enoch, "I'll make them sorry."

"What about Gyp? Where's he? I wish he'd come see me now and then. I do like that boy."

"I reckon he's at home," said Enoch. "I haven't seen him since school let out this afternoon."

"Tell him about the pie, too," said Luddie Belle.

Enoch smiled.

"I tell you another favorite of mine," said Luddie Belle. "That little Billy Boy. He's a sweetie-pie, ain't he? He and them two little twins. They're the funniest crew I ever seen. Now, Effie, she don't seem like the other three. It's like she was cut from different cloth, flighty as she is."

"But I kind of like Effie," said Enoch. "She's got her good points."

"Why, of course she has. But Effie's not like her brothers. It seems like she's too preoccupied with herself. But that's often the case with the oldest child."

Enoch did not say anything. Self-consciously he turned his attention to the pie.

64

A moment of silence passed.

"Of course, here you sit, the oldest one of the whole bunch," said Luddie Belle.

"That's right," said Enoch.

"The big brother of them all."

"Sort of like that," said Enoch.

"I understand you're thinking of going away," said Luddie Belle. "Betty told me something about it."

Enoch shrugged. "It's something I've been thinking about. I can go live with my uncle next fall if I want."

Luddie Belle sighed.

"I haven't decided yet," said Enoch. "I might not go."

Luddie Belle shook her head. "We seen it happen so many times, young-uns grow up and move away. All mine are gone. I tell you, there was a time there when it looked like this whole town was going to die. Looked like there wasn't going to be nobody left but us old folks. Then you new people showed up. First Kate and Morgan. Of course, Kate grew up here, but she had been off to college, you know. Then your mama and daddy came along. Then the Nashes and the McCalls and the others. Now I'll admit, there was folks around here weren't so keen on it at first. I'll even admit I was one of them. We weren't used to this kind of young folks. But we got to know them a little bit and they seemed nice, not like what we'd expected. And they was willing to work." She paused. "But then I reckon I shouldn't be talking like this to you. About your own people and all." She smiled and put her hand on Enoch's arm. "You'll have to excuse an old lady's rambling."

"It don't bother me," said Enoch, although it did a little.

Suddenly Luddie Belle laughed and sat back in her chair. "Do you remember the Stroupes rolling into town?"

Enoch shook his head.

"Land o' love, what a sight that was. They came in from California driving this—I don't know what you'd call it—looked like an old bookmobile. Had rainbows painted all over it."

"I remember that van," said Enoch.

"Bud had the most hair I ever seen on a man. And Betty floating around in a long dress, bright-colored, hair down to her waist. And little Gladys, dirty as a street urchin, clinging to her skirts. Except they called Gladys by some funny name back then."

"Galadriel," said Enoch. "They named her for an elf queen in a book."

"Did you ever." Luddie Belle was laughing.

"Nobody could pronounce it," said Enoch. "I think it was Bert McPhee who started calling her Gladys. At least, that's the story."

"Probably was Bert," said Luddie Belle. "That was after they'd bought the building in town and set up their business. Now, that set the town on its ear for a while, I can tell you."

"What did? Buying the building?"

"Whoo-oo," cackled Luddie. "You should've heard the telephones buzzing. The hippies were going to take over the town, folks were saying. Going to buy us out. Let me tell you, it wouldn't have taken much to do it. They bought that old building for two thousand dollars. For ten they could've had the town."

Enoch laughed.

"I think it was Joe Stokes who made the difference," said Luddie Belle.

"Mountain Man, you mean," said Enoch.

"I know that's what you-uns call him," said Luddie Belle. "But Joe Stokes is the name he was born with—up there on Jenkins Ridge. I knew his mama.' Luddie Belle paused. "Now what was I saying?"

"About the Stroupes," said Enoch.

"That's right. The Stroupes. They moved in here and got everybody in a tizzie, and it was Joe that went around and talked to a few people and calmed them down. And from what I heard, he was the one talked Bud into shaving off that beard and trimming back his hair a little. I know it don't seem like much now, but back then it made us all feel better. Made us feel like these new people had some respect for our ways, if you know what I mean."

Enoch nodded.

"Of course, we got to where we all liked them. I wouldn't take anything for that Gladys. And that little Bubba. They gave him a funny name, too, didn't they?"

"Meriadoc."

"I knew it was something like that. Sometimes I wonder if it was getting a name like that that's made him so shy."

"Well, I've heard people say it's having Gladys for a big sister," said Enoch. "Her being so outgoing and all. But it don't seem right, somehow, throwing off on Gladys that way."

"No, it don't," said Luddie. "Each child born is different, each with its own quirks, you might say. I like that little Bubba, when I can get him to talk to me."

"He'll talk if you get him in the right situation," said Enoch. "He's a nice little kid."

"Him and Gladys both. Us old-timers, we like having

them young-uns around. We like having a bakery, too, and that restaurant. Why, Mattie Fitzgerald's even taken to eating alfalfa sprouts." She laughed. "Did you ever? Alfalfa sprouts."

Enoch smiled and nodded. "They're good on sandwiches," he said, pushing back his chair. He stood up and stretched. "I reckon I'd better be going."

"You're not going to finish that pie?"

He patted his stomach. "It was good, but you gave me too much."

Luddie Belle looked at him. "So you really are going away, Enoch. When Betty told me that, I near about cried. All this time I'd been thinking you young-uns were going to be different. I thought you were going to be the ones to stay."

"Well," Enoch said regretfully. "It's not certain yet. I'll be making my decision this summer."

"Oh, pooh. You've done made it and you know it. I don't know why I keep letting myself get attached to young-uns. A place like Swallowfield can't hold them. They always leave in the end."

Enoch looked at her apologetically, not knowing what to say. He turned and started toward the front door. Luddie Belle followed him.

"Thanks again for my milk," she said.

"Sure," he said opening the door and going out. "I was glad to do it."

Luddie Belle stood in the doorway, watching him go down the steps.

"And don't mind an old woman's prattle," she said. "You go ahead and do what you have to do. Even if it's wrong."

Enoch laughed and looked at her over his shoulder. She was smiling. He untied Reno and mounted from the bumper of the car. Then he waved and rode out of the yard onto the gravel road and down the hill. He knew that she stood and watched him until he was out of sight.

FIVE

Rita. She lived in an old cabin halfway up Wolf Ridge on the back of Bill and Melinda Nash's property at the head of the valley. The headwaters of Kettle Creek trickled by her doorstep. She lived alone and liked it that way. A hundred feet from her house, where the footpath approached a spur of the hill that hid her cabin from view, a rope hung down from an oak tree. Attached to the rope was a sign that read: DOORBELL—PULL HARD. Pulleys hanging from tree limbs carried the rope to Rita's front yard, where it was fastened to a bucket with rocks inside. Rita sometimes went naked around her place, and the doorbell was to give her time to get dressed.

The thought of it drove Enoch crazy. He was in love with Rita. The fact that she was twenty-six years old made no difference to him. He was in love with her unfettered spirit and in love with her voluptuous body. Especially her body. And most of all her large, bouncy breasts. Because of his love for Rita the doorbell in the trees was a torture. Its very existence made him imagine going up to her house without ringing it. He daydreamed about it all the time. Once he had even gone so far as to ride Reno up through the woods on the hill behind Rita's house, hoping to steal a glimpse of her. But she was not outside to be seen and he had felt ashamed of himself for trying it. He worried that she might have seen him, and this made him even more ashamed. So he did not try anything like that anymore.

Being in love with Rita was not easy. It was agony, a delicious agony. She, of course, knew nothing of his feelings, and Enoch meant to keep it that way. He shared his secret with no one. He was not a fool. He understood the impossibility of it. He knew the reality of the eleven years between them. And he knew the reality of Bo: Bo the strong and handsome, the Louisiana man, the romantic rambler with the ready smile and crinkly eyes. Enoch hated him. Every year, like the spring wind, Bo breezed through the valley on his way north from the sunny lands where he had wintered. He would stay with Rita for a month or two before moving on to Canada or New England for the summer. In the fall he would return, stay a time, and then head south just ahead of the cold weather. He was well liked on Kettle Creek. All but Enoch were glad to see him come and sorry to see him go. They never knew exactly when he would show up or how he would arrive. Sometimes he hitchhiked in. One year he drove up in an ancient '47 Chevrolet. This year he came by bus.

It was the middle of March, a school day. Enoch and Mercy left home at quarter to nine and walked up the valley to the Nashes'. Billy Boy Nash came bounding down the steps of the two-room schoolhouse, proud to be the first one to tell them that Bo was coming. But Enoch turned away at the news, not wanting to hear the details. His day was ruined. His whole spring was ruined.

"Didn't you hear, Enoch?" said Mercy. "Bo's coming."

"Good," said Enoch, barely hiding his feelings from these children who were too young to understand.

"Don't you want to hear about it?" said Billy Boy.

"What's there to hear?"

"There's going to be a party," said Billy Boy. "Tonight. Here in our yard. We're going to have a bonfire and music and dancing."

"When's he coming?" said Mercy. "When's he getting here?" She was excited.

"About suppertime," said Billy Boy. "He's coming on a bus. Rita's going to meet him in Fairmont. At five o'clock. That's when he gets there. He told it all to Mama on the telephone this morning. Effie's gone up to tell Rita."

Enoch stepped impatiently around Billy Boy and Mercy and went into the schoolhouse. Melinda was inside getting ready for a day of teaching. Dee and Dum were chasing each other around the desks. Seeing Enoch, they swerved toward him.

"Enoch! Enoch! Bo's coming! Bo's coming!" they cried and began chasing around him.

"Oh, god," muttered Enoch, turning to leave.

Melinda looked up. "Morning, Enoch. Anything wrong?"

"Not really," said Enoch. "I reckon I'm just not in the mood for little kids this morning."

"Roland. Robbie," said Melinda to the twins. They kept chasing around, paying no attention.

Enoch laughed. He could not help it. "Hey, Dee, Dum," he said and caught each one by his collar. "Your mama's calling you."

72

The two little boys looked around at Melinda. She sighed. "Go on outside," she told them. "We need a little peace in here."

"Yeah, look," said Enoch, turning them around so they could see out the door. "Yonder comes Gyp and Liddle."

The twins broke for the door, stopping on the porch to holler out that Bo was coming and then hurrying down the steps.

Enoch smiled. "They never will know their real names."

"If you'd all quit this Tweedledee and Tweedledum business, they would," Melinda said irritably. "How would you like to be Dum and suddenly get old enough to find out that your name means stupid? That's going to happen, you know."

"Oh, it doesn't mean stupid," said Enoch. "It might sound like 'dumb,' but it's not spelled the same or anything. It's like Mountain Man says. When you call somebody 'dear,' they don't think you're calling them an animal with big brown eyes and antlers."

"It's not the same," said Melinda. "And anyway, they're my kids, aren't they? Why shouldn't a mother have the say-so over her own children's names?"

"Seems like names around here get a life of their own," said Enoch. "I've tried calling Dum Robbie, but I just can't. It doesn't seem . . . I don't know. It just don't sound loving enough."

Melinda smiled. "That's sweet, Enoch."

Enoch turned away to his desk, half wishing he had not said it.

Gyp came inside.

"Hey, Enoch. How about old Bo coming in? And a party tonight? Pretty good, huh?"

"Yeah, that's great," said Enoch, trying to seem genuinely pleased. Gyp was the hardest one to deceive. Enoch almost had to fool himself to do it.

Gyp sat down on a table near the wood stove and began flipping a pencil in the air.

Effie came in. She was somewhat breathless but nonetheless composed, moving with measured, graceful steps, tossing her long blond hair with calculated drama. She was eleven, a year older than Mercy and Liddle, and was lately obsessed with the idea of becoming an actress.

"I told Rita, Mother," she said with a flourish. "I had to wake her up."

Enoch's nostrils flared at the thought, and his mind grew numb. If only he could have been sent. He reached into his desk and took out a book and opened it and stared at it. What might the day have held for him if he had been the one sent to Rita's?

He looked up and gazed out the window and saw Bill Nash, the other teacher, coming across the yard from the house. Bill disappeared from the view of the window and reappeared in the doorway.

"Morning, everybody," Bill said. Then to Enoch and Gyp he said, "How's it going, fellas?"

"Pretty good," said Gyp.

"Fine," said Enoch, and he stared at his book again, trying not to give anything away. Bill was another one who knew him too well.

"How about it, Effie?" said Bill. "Did you give Rita the word?"

"Yes, Father," said Effie, the actress delivering her lines. "She was supposed to do some painting today for Sarah Duke, but it's outside work and she can put it off until tomorrow."

"Bo can help her tomorrow," said Gyp. "Get it done twice as fast."

Enoch looked up irritably from his book. Maybe Bo would take a wrong bus and end up in Alaska.

Then he felt Bill looking at him. He glanced in Bill's direction, and as their eyes met, Enoch spoke quickly to cover himself.

"Big party tonight, huh?" he said, putting enthusiasm in his voice.

"Rites of spring," said Bill, and for a moment his eyes still rested on Enoch. Then he looked around at the others. "When Bo comes, you know winter's over."

"Listen, folks," said Melinda, holding up the book she had been trying to read. "Either let's get school started or y'all clear out and let me study."

"Gladys and them aren't here yet," said Effie.

"Then let me have a little quiet," said Melinda.

"A little quiet for Melinda," said Bill, and he went back outside.

Effie followed him.

"Come on," Gyp said to Enoch.

"You go if you want," said Enoch. "I got some stuff to look over."

"What stuff?"

"That algebra."

"What? You've been helping *me* with algebra. You know it backwards and forwards."

Enoch gave up. There was no refuge, no way to be alone with his torment.

"I guess I've got it down good enough," he said, getting up and following Gyp outside.

The Stroupes' van, not the old rainbow one but a newer,

75

more conservative one, was bouncing up the driveway, Billy Boy running to meet it. Betty was driving, and Gladys and Bubba were on the seat beside her. As the van rolled to a stop, the side door opened and out piled half the Kettle Creek school—Mary Lou and Janie McCall, Bethie and Steve Iverson, and the three Flint Creek kids, Flower, Ezekiel, and Fred. Gladys got out of the front and turned and held out her arms to Bubba.

"Come on, Bubba," she said. "Don't you want to go to school today?"

Bubba shook his head and moved closer to Betty.

"We'll have fun, Bubba. Dee and Dum are here. They go to school every day and they're littler than you."

Bubba shook his head firmly.

"Mama, can't you *make* him come? I know he'd do better. He'd talk more and everything if he'd just come on and join in."

"No," Bubba said quietly.

Betty sighed. "I don't want to force him, Gladys. You didn't go to school when you were four."

"Because we didn't have Bill and Melinda's school, that's why."

"Well, today's not the day he's going to change his mind," said Betty. "Run along. You're holding things up. Be good."

"Okay, Bubba," said Gladys. "You win again. Bye-bye, squirt."

Bubba smiled. "Bye," he said.

"Bye, Mama," said Gladys, and she shut the van door and headed for the schoolhouse.

Enoch and Gyp were waiting in front for her.

"Bubba's hopeless," said Gladys as they started up the steps.

"Never mind Bubba," said Gyp. "Bo's coming in today. There's going to be a party tonight."

"Bo!" said Gladys. "Hot diggity." And she went dancing inside ahead of them.

Enoch felt sick at his stomach.

The sick feeling stayed with him through algebra and then history, surging through him with every thought of Bo and Rita. Bo in her house, Bo alone with her, sharing her meals, sharing her work, sharing her bed, that one bed. There was not even a couch he might be using, not a chance he was sleeping anywhere but in her bed, under the covers with her, for a month, two months, and then he would be off, leaving her, just like that, without a thought. Obviously Bo did not love her, nor she him. If he did, he would not leave so easily, and if she loved him, she would not seem so content to be alone. But why did he always come back? And why did she always welcome him? Why Bo, when it was Enoch who loved her so much? The unfairness rankled him: that it should be Bo coming today to share her house and her bed, to be where Enoch so longed to be.

The morning finally passed, and it was time for lunch. As Enoch was getting up to leave, Melinda came over to him.

"Are you feeling all right?" she said.

"I'm okay," said Enoch. "I guess maybe I've got a cold coming on or something. I feel a little off. It's nothing bad."

He took his lunch and went out and wandered off across the driveway and through the newly tilled garden to the Nashes' pasture. Leaning his elbows on the gate, he nibbled without appetite at his sandwich and watched the Nashes' new flock of sheep. He was thinking about going home.

He glanced back at the schoolhouse and noticed Bill Nash coming toward him through the garden. Enoch turned back to the sheep. Maybe Bill was just checking to see if his seeds had sprouted yet. Enoch had noticed some new peas coming up.

But he heard Bill's footsteps coming on until they were right behind him. Enoch looked around.

"I'm not disturbing you, am I?" said Bill.

"No," said Enoch.

Bill came up and leaned on the gate beside him. He glanced at Enoch's half-eaten sandwich.

"Looks like you're off your feed," he said.

"It's not a very good sandwich," said Enoch.

"Anything wrong?" said Bill. "Anything you want to talk about?"

Enoch looked out at the sheep. There was a time when he could tell Bill anything, when every problem that came up was a thing to be shared. But this with Rita was different.

"No," he said. "There's nothing." He took a bite of his sandwich and chewed it slowly, still staring at the sheep.

"Pretty nice flock, wouldn't you say?" said Bill.

"Yeah, they look good to me," said Enoch. "Course, I'm no expert on sheep. These are the first ones I've ever seen close up."

"You and me both," said Bill.

"The ewes are getting fatter," said Enoch.

"They're supposed to start lambing in about two weeks."

"Are y'all ready for that?" said Enoch. "I've always heard it's tricky. And a lot of work."

78

"The guy we bought them from said he'd come help us with the first one or two, until we get the hang of it. Come watch if you want. We'll be glad to put you to work."

"If it's not in the middle of the night, I might," said Enoch.

"Well, they say that's usually when it is," said Bill.

"With cows, too," said Enoch. "It'd be nice if they'd all drop their calves around two in the afternoon. But usually it's more like one in the morning."

"There must be some reason for it," said Bill. "Some evolutionary principle."

"I reckon," said Enoch, straightening up from the gate.

"I guess we better be getting back," said Bill.

Enoch looked at the uneaten sandwich in his hand.

"Mollie'll eat it for you," said Bill.

"That's a good idea," said Enoch, and he whistled for the dog.

Enoch and Mercy and Lizzie sat on the porch steps watching the sun go down behind Brokeleg Mountain. Mercy and Lizzie were talking, but Enoch sat a little apart from them. As he stroked Petunia, who was curled in his lap, he looked out at the fading sky and watched a distant flock of birds heading north.

D. J. and Wanda came walking up the road. They stopped in front of the house and waved up the hill.

"Y'all coming to the party?" D. J. called.

"Waiting for Clark," Lizzie called back. "Be along in a little."

"He working?"

"At the sawmill."

D. J. looked away from them and shifted from one foot to

79

the other. Then he reached up and tilted his leather hat forward on his head and looked back up at them from beneath the brim.

"See you up there," he called and waved again. Wanda waved, too, and the Callahans waved back.

"I guess Drawing Jack's forgotten what it's like to work," Lizzie muttered.

"I don't think he's too proud of getting fired from the mill," said Enoch.

Lizzie did not take it up.

For a few moments they sat quietly, watching the valley. Then Enoch cocked his head toward the road, listening.

"Who's coming?" asked Mercy.

Enoch listened, not saying anything, watching the bend in the road as an ancient green pickup truck bobbed into view.

"It's Rita," cried Mercy, jumping to her feet. "Rita and Bo." She began waving her arms. From the window of the passenger side of the truck a man's arm came out and waved back.

"Let's go see them," said Mercy, bouncing around in excitement. "Let's go down to the road and meet them."

"We'll see them at the party," said Enoch.

"I'm going to go see them now," said Mercy. "I'll be the first one to see Bo." And she was off down the hill. The truck stopped and waited for her. She jumped onto the running board on Rita's side, and Enoch watched sullenly as Bo's arm reached across Rita and his big hand tousled Mercy's hair. Rita spoke and Mercy turned toward the house.

"Mama," she called, "I'm going to ride up with them."

"See you later," called Lizzie, waving. Rita's door

opened and Enoch felt a rush as Mercy clambered across Rita's lap into the space between her and Bo. The truck started rolling again, and they were gone.

"Here's Clark," said Lizzie, and Enoch turned and saw the red truck turning into the driveway. He had not even heard it until now.

As Clark parked the truck in the yard and got out, Lizzie got to her feet.

"I hope you're not too tired for a party," she said. "Bo's back."

"Old Bo," said Clark with a smile. "As regular as the swallows of Capistrano. Where's the party?"

"At the Nashes'," said Lizzie.

"Just let me take a quick shower," said Clark. He started up the steps by Enoch. "How's it going, old buddy," he said, clapping him on the shoulder. "You're looking kind of down."

"Nah," said Enoch. "I'm all right. Maybe a little hungry is all."

They walked to the Nashes', starting out in dusky darkness, Clark with his guitar slung across his back, Enoch with a bowl of coleslaw cradled in one arm, and Soupy the dog trotting along in front of them. The Harrimans' house, when they passed it, was dark. But farther on, at Mountain Man's, they saw a light. As they approached, the light went out and they heard Mountain Man's front door open and close. They stopped and waited, watching his tall, round-shouldered figure amble down the gravel driveway. He was carrying a case of beer on one shoulder.

"You got the essentials," said Clark as Mountain Man reached them.

"Yep," said Mountain Man. "The rest'll take care of itself."

They walked on up the road and came to the Nashes' part of the valley. Mountain Man stopped and looked across the pasture, the white forms of the sheep still visible in the gathering darkness.

"Bill's going to lose his shirt on them sheep," he said.

"He says he's lost it on everything else, he might as well try sheep," said Lizzie.

They laughed, as at an old joke.

"He's not cut out for farming, that's for sure," said Clark as they moved on down the road.

"Nope," said Mountain Man. "He won't stay on it, is why. Ain't nothing you can raise that's going to take care of itself. You got to be there when you're needed, get the weeds before they get up so, pick the tomatoes before they turn too ripe to market, notice an animal the first day it gets sick, not three days later. But Bill, he's always got his mind on something else he's doing. Tries to farm with one hand. That don't never work."

"But he's a good teacher," said Enoch.

"Hell, yes, he is," said Mountain Man. "Wouldn't trade him for the whole Massey County school system. All I'm saying is, I feel sorry for them sheep."

Enoch laughed. "If they only knew what happened to the chickens. Hawks and foxes picked them off one at a time."

"One at a time? Hell, one night he lost *six*. All of them good layers, too."

They had come now to the cars and trucks parked in and around the Nashes' driveway and were threading their way through them in the darkness. In the yard between the house and the schoolhouse a small fire was burning. A few people were squatting around it roasting weiners. Enoch looked closely to see who they were. On the far side of the fire, with light flickering on their faces, were Gladys, Donovan, and Effie. There were two people on the near side, a man and a woman. He could only see their backs in silhouette, but after a moment's study he knew they were Brandy and Stuart, not Rita and Bo. Maybe those two were in the house. Usually there was a crowd in the kitchen. Enoch handed the bowl of coleslaw to Clark.

"You want to take this in?" he said. "I'm going to go cook me a hot dog." He started over to the fire. But then two people he had not noticed left the bench under the apple tree and headed for the fire. Rita and Bo: even by their shadows Enoch knew them. He turned aside, unable to go forward to meet them. He went back to the parked cars, as if he had some business there, and then circled around, picking his way through the darkness to the back of the schoolhouse, far from people. He sat down on the big rock that was there by the fence, wishing he had not come, wishing he had pretended to be sick and had stayed at home. He was not going to be able to face Bo this year. He knew it now. His jealousy had grown too great.

For a long time he sat on the rock, and listened to the voices and the laughter, and smelled the smoke and the weiners cooking. He felt hungry and miserable and foolish. Thoughts of Rita washed over him—tender, sensual thoughts and jealous, angry ones. After a while came the music, the sweet whine of Brandy's fiddle warming up, and the tender thoughts grew stronger, saddening him. He listened to the strumming and plunking of Clark's guitar as he tuned it. And now Stuart was starting in on his mandolin and Donovan on his banjo. This was the warm, loving time that was beginning—the music, the people close around. But Enoch remained alone in the dark, aching and throbbing, cursing the Louisiana man.

Then out of the darkness came footsteps, startlingly close. Enoch felt his face flushing, burning with embarrassment. He did not want to be found here, did not want to explain himself. In the shadows by the schoolhouse he could see a lighter shadow moving, a single form, man-sized, big like Bo. It was the worst thing, the worst possible thing that could happen. Enoch shrank into himself, trying to hide without moving. He could not really see Bo, only the movement of him as he approached.

"How's it going, Enoch?" The voice was Bill Nash's, not Bo's at all. Enoch let out his breath, not realizing he had been holding it.

"Okay," he said, and in his relief his embarrassment drained away.

"Still not feeling sociable, huh?"

"Not too," Enoch said quietly.

Bill came toward him holding out both hands, offering something. Enoch looked closely and saw a hot dog and a can of beer.

"Hey, thanks," he said, reaching for them, glad now that Bill had come.

"Don't get drunk," said Bill. "You'll get me in trouble."

"Nah," said Enoch. "They don't care if I have a beer or two."

Bill sat down on the ground and leaned back against a fence post. "The music sounds nice from out here," he said. "Kind of soft and melancholy."

"Too melancholy," said Enoch, wanting to convey meaning, but not too much meaning. Bill said nothing, and in the silence Enoch felt easy. They listened as the band started in on "John Hardy." Mountain Man was playing his harmonica on this one, and people were singing. When the last verse came, Bill sang along softly.

I been to the east and I been to the west,
I traveled this wide world round,
I been to the river and I been baptized,
So take me to my hanging ground, Lord, Lord;
So take me to my hanging ground.

For another moment they were silent.

Then Bill said, "What are your thoughts about Raleigh these days?"

"You mean, am I going?"

"That's what I'm getting at."

"Officially, I haven't decided. But if you want to know the truth, I'm going."

Bill was quiet. He picked up a long twig and slowly broke small pieces from it until it was gone.

Then he said, "Enoch, have you ever thought of staying here and going to high school in Fairmont?"

Enoch shook his head. "That's no place," he said. "A country school in the boonies is all it is. Yours and Melinda's school is better. At least we learn things."

"It's better for some things maybe," said Bill. "But not for others."

"Like what?"

"Like girls."

Enoch took a drink of beer. Bill knew. He knew about Rita and why Enoch was sitting out here. Enoch was embarrassed, but glad in a way.

"Fairmont girls aren't much," he said. "I know a few of them. Nothing to get excited about."

"Then you don't know the right ones," said Bill. "If I were you, I'd try school in Fairmont before I went off to live in a city."

"I got other reasons for going to Raleigh besides girls," said Enoch. "Lots of reasons."

"Like."

"It's complicated."

"Too complicated to talk about?"

Enoch nodded. "I tried to explain it to Clark and Lizzie, but I couldn't really. I don't think I could get you to understand either."

Bill sat quietly for a moment.

"Maybe not," he said and picked up another twig and broke it away piece by piece.

Then he stood up. "You want to come back and join the party? Folks are going to start wondering where you are."

"I guess so," said Enoch, getting to his feet. "I could use a little more food."

When they got back to the party, the fire was blazing brighter and the yard was full of people. The band was playing "Old Joe Clark" and there were people dancing, clogging in the old mountain way. Enoch stood and watched Mercy dance, her feet expertly stomping and tapping to the music, her hands clapping, her face happy. When she saw Enoch, she held out her hand to him, inviting him to dance. He moved in and joined the cloggers, the music carrying him along, touching something deep in him, something old. His turmoil gave way before it, and for the brief time that the music played on he was happy.

Then it ended, and there was laughter and clapping

as the dancers slumped over to the sidelines. Enoch started toward the food table. Then someone touched his shoulder and he turned around.

"Put it here, hoss," said Bo, holding out his hand.

Enoch's breath stopped in his chest, but he managed to shake Bo's hand.

"How you been," said Bo.

"All right," said Enoch, finding his breath again, his eyes sweeping to Rita, lovely Rita, standing by Bo. To his numbed senses she seemed suspended in space, glowing against the vacant darkness. He dragged his eyes back to Bo. "How about you?" he managed to say.

"Had a good winter," said Bo. "Stayed down in Mexico part of the time. Then I went to Florida."

"Oh?" said Enoch, trying not to look at Rita. He felt stupid and awkward. "Pretty warm down, there, I guess."

Bo smiled. "Warm enough," he said.

Enoch shifted. He could think of nothing to say, nothing at all. He panicked, not wanting to seem tongue-tied.

"Reckon I'll go stir up a little grub," he blurted, then stood awkwardly for a moment, stealing a look at her, his eyes skimming the front of her jacket, searching for curves.

"Got to think about your stomach," Bo said, good-naturedly. "Be talking to you later."

"Sure, later," said Enoch, the words thick and clumsy, and he turned and walked away on Donald Duck feet.

When his mind cleared, he found himself standing in front of the food table. He felt awful. She must have seen him as a fool, a young, awkward fool of a kid. If only he had still been holding the beer Bill had given him. That would have been better—to have stood there loose and relaxed, swilling down some beer. He would do that next time. He

87

ought to keep a beer in his hand at all times, just in case. He went looking for the beer, still slightly befuddled. The band was taking a break. People were milling around. Then he heard her voice.

"Over here, Enoch."

He looked and saw her by the fire. Mercy, Liddle, and Effie were beside her. Gyp was there, too, and the other kids, all of them, and Bo was in their midst. Enoch hesitated, then walked over slowly. Grown-ups were gathering around.

"Come on, Enoch," said Rita and motioned for him to come closer to where she and Bo and the children were. Enoch had a dreadful feeling. He moved forward reluctantly.

"You'll never believe the job I had in Florida this winter," Bo was saying, and he seemed to be speaking more to the children than to the grown-ups. "Feeding lions, and exercising an elephant, and doing an engine overhaul on a little bitty clown car."

"A circus!" cried Billy Boy.

"That's right," said Bo. "An honest-to-goodness circus, wintering in Florida. And it's going to play in Asheville this summer. I just happen to have some tickets here, and Rita promises to get you all there when the time comes."

The younger children cheered and jumped around, holding out their hands, and Rita and Bo started passing out the tickets. Enoch began to back away in horror. Now Rita was giving one to Gyp, who was not jumping around but was grinning nonetheless and taking the ticket gratefully.

"One more," said Bo, holding up the last ticket. "Who doesn't have one?"

Enoch was back among the grown-ups, trying to blend in.

"Where's Enoch?" said Mercy, looking around. "Hey, Bo. I bet it's Enoch's." Enoch started to turn and flee. But people were looking at him. Effie was pointing to him. Bo was coming toward him with the ticket. And Rita was there, watching it all.

"Here you go, Enoch," said Bo, and he handed the ticket toward him.

"Nah," said Enoch, putting up his hand in nonchalant refusal. "Save it and give it to a kid."

"No, this one's yours," said Bo and he put it into his hand. Enoch did not want it. His hand did not want to take it. But to refuse it that way, to let it fall away to the ground, that would reveal too much. With a groan inside himself his fingers closed around it. He looked at Rita. She was watching, beaming with approval as her Louisiana man gave circus tickets to the children.

SIX

Rita turned off the paved road onto the rough dirt road of the valley, the truck's headlights flitting over the tractor standing silent in the dark sorghum field. In the afternoon when she was driving Bo to Fairmont to catch the bus, they had seen Enoch on the tractor. He had been concentrating so hard on his cultivating that he did not even see them as they drove past, did not look up to see them and wave good-by, though he knew that this was the day Bo was leaving. They had noticed it. They had commented on how intent he was on his work, on steering the tractor along the rows, keeping the blades of the cultivator in line and away from the young sorghum plants, so intent that he did not even look up and wave.

Now Rita could see lamplight inside the Callahan house. That would be Enoch and Lizzie. Clark and Mercy would be with the others at the bluegrass festival, sixty miles away, camping all night, with more music through tomorrow. She knew it was Lizzie and Enoch's turn to stay home with the cows.

The Harrimans were gone, their house dark, as were Mountain Man's and Bill and Melinda's. The valley seemed lonesome. The truck seemed lonesome without Bo sitting there beside her as she bounced up the last leg of the rutted driveway, going up as far as she could go and parking beneath the trees. She got out and started up the path, carrying no light because she needed none. She was aware of the darkness and quietness, felt it more than usual because for two months now Bo had been with her on this path, but now he was on the bus, rolling away to the north, and she was alone. So she was noticing more than ever the quietness of the night, and perhaps that was why she heard the groan. She turned and listened and heard nothing more.

But she was sure she had heard it. She went back to the truck and got a flashlight and shone it into the darkness beyond the pasture fence. It was Bill and Melinda's pasture, where they kept the sheep, but she saw no sheep, no animal of any kind. Yet she was sure she had heard it. A groan. A suffering sound. She climbed the fence and went looking, scanning with the light across the pasture until she found the ewe.

Rita knew nothing about lambing. Bill and Melinda had handled it all when the other ewes had lambed. This was the newest ewe, the one that was bred later than the others, the one she had heard Bill say was due next week. So Bill and Melinda were off on a lark and Rita, who knew nothing about lambing, was here with the ewe, and the ewe was in trouble. She could see it, the two tiny legs protruding from the birth canal, but the ewe was not straining, just lying

91

there quiet and still, and breathing hard as if she had been trying and trying but now had given up.

"Jesus, sheep," muttered Rita. "You poor thing. Hang on while I go get Lizzie." And then she was off across the pasture and over the fence, leaping into the truck, and racing down the dirt road to the Callahans'.

It was the first time Enoch had ever been left in charge at home overnight. At the last minute Clark and Lizzie had decided he was old enough for it, and they had gone together to the festival, leaving Enoch and Mercy with the cows. Gyp was there too. They all three heard Rita's truck and ran out to the porch.

"Anything wrong?" asked Enoch as Rita jumped out of the truck.

"Where's Lizzie?" said Rita.

"At the festival," said Enoch. "Is something wrong?"

"Is Clark here?"

"No, they're both gone. What's wrong?"

"Nobody's here? You're here alone?"

"Yeah. What is it? What's happened?"

"Jesus, I can't believe this," said Rita. She stood with her hands on her hips, looking away into the night. "Where's the nearest vet?"

"Fairmont," said Gyp.

"It's that last ewe," said Rita. "She's lambing and she's having trouble."

"It'd take forever to get the vet out here," said Gyp.

"I've helped with calves," said Enoch.

"Are they like sheep?" said Rita.

"Probably," said Enoch. "If the lamb's hung up, we'll have to reach up inside and straighten it out."

"That's what I was afraid of," said Rita. "Have you ever done that with a calf?"

"I watched Clark and Lizzie do it once. A leg got caught. They had to kind of push the calf back in before they could get the caught leg loose and get both legs coming out together."

"This one's already got two legs out."

"Then maybe she was just resting," said Gyp. "Maybe when we get back up there, she'll have the rest of it out."

"We've got a book," said Enoch. "We'll take it with us. And we've got to have flashlights. And towels. And dish soap. Liquid soap. That's what Clark and Lizzie used to make their hands slide in. And a big jug of water for scrubbing up."

"Let's hurry," said Mercy, running into the house to gather the things together.

Then the truck was bouncing up the road again, the four of them crowded into the cab, and Gyp was reading to them by flashlight from the book.

"It says here the two front feet usually come out first," he said.

"That's how it is with cows," said Enoch.

"Then about the time you get to the knees, the nose comes out,"

"That's right," said Enoch. "Like cows."

"There wasn't any nose with these legs," said Rita. "Not that I noticed."

"Maybe it was back legs," said Enoch. "I've helped pull out backward calves before. They don't usually get stuck though. They just need more help to get breathing fast."

"Or . . ." said Gyp, holding his finger to the text, trying to read against the jouncing, "or the head might be caught

93

back. Sometimes the two front legs come out, but the head turns back inside the uterus. Look here at the picture."

Rita was too busy driving, so he showed it to Enoch and Mercy. "It's like this," Mercy said to Rita, and she held her arms together straight out in front and turned her face back over her shoulder, closing her eyes to look more like the unborn lamb and tilting back her head to show it was caught.

"That might be it," said Rita. "What does it say to do?"

"Wait a minute," said Gyp, and he read ahead. They were alongside the pasture now, and Rita was slowing down, looking for the right place to stop. "You stick your hand in and find the head," said Gyp. "You feel up the legs to the shoulders and then to the head, and you have to be careful it's not the head of a twin. Sheep lots of times have twins."

"Oh, lord," muttered Rita.

"Okay, so you find the head. Then you use your other hand to take hold of the front legs and push the lamb back in a little. That's to give you room to get the head around. Then you cup your hand around behind the head and try to pull it around and get its nose pointed into the birth canal along with the legs."

Rita parked the truck and turned off the engine. "Let me see that picture," she said, and Gyp gave it to her with the flashlight. She studied it. "All right," she said at last, handing the book back to Gyp. "I guess we can do it. But bring the book."

"Everybody move quietly," said Enoch. "And talk soft. Sheep scare easy."

They found the ewe again, and she was like she was before except that now Rita could see that she was still strain-

94

ing, though only now and then. Rita held the light, and she and Enoch got down and studied the situation, Gyp and Mercy leaning over them from behind.

"Okay now," Rita said quietly. "We've got two legs, right?"

"And they're front ones because the bottoms of the feet are down," said Enoch. "That's how you tell. Back ones are turned up. At least in cows."

"With sheep, too," said Gyp. "The book said."

"Okay," said Rita, taking a breath, trying to stay composed. "Two front feet and no head. We've got to go in and find the head." She stood up. "Where's the soap and water?"

"Here," said Mercy and fetched her the water jug and the soap and towel. Gyp sat down on the ground with a flashlight and opened the book.

"Think you can do it, Rita?" said Enoch.

"I'll try," she said.

"It says here to be calm and take your time," said Gyp. "That's important. Just feel around first and figure out where everything is. Try to feel if there's twins or not."

"Jesus, be calm," said Rita, lathering her hands furiously. "Working on the truck I can be calm. But this is an animal. A lady animal. Like me. She feels things. She could die. She probably will die."

"No," said Enoch. "We can help her."

"Bill and Melinda should be here, damn their eyes. They should have known she was ready. They don't know a god-damn thing about sheep."

"You want me to try to do it?" said Enoch.

"No, I'm ready," said Rita. "I'm calm, I really am. Pretty calm. Just blowing off a little at getting stuck with this. I've

95

never even watched anybody do anything like this."

"But I have," said Enoch. "It'll be all right. You want me to try it?"

"No, here I go," said Rita, coating her hand now with the liquid soap. "You hold her and keep her still. Mercy, you hold the light for me. Gyp, you man the book."

"Just go in easy," said Gyp.

Rita knelt behind the ewe and placed her fingers on the two little protruding legs and then began sliding her hand up into the warmth of the ewe. "Okay," she said softly. "I'm doing it. I can feel where the legs end, so here's the shoulders. Now, back here must be . . . no, not on that side. Around here . . . yeah . . . okay . . . here's the head. I found it."

"Make sure it's not the twin's head," said Enoch.

"How?"

"Feel all around. See if there's another lamb in there. See where its head is."

"Yeah," said Gyp. "It says sometimes twins get tangled and try to both come out at once. It don't work."

"Okay," said Rita. "I'm looking," and she pushed her hand further in, feeling, and for several moments there was no sound except the ewe's breathing and Rita's, and then she said, "There's not another one. There's nothing else but this one. So that's okay. Now, if I can find the head again. Back here somewhere. Yeah, here it is. Okay. This isn't so bad once you learn your way around. I'm going to try to turn it now."

"Push in the legs," said Enoch.

"Oh yeah," said Rita, and she grasped the protruding legs with her free hand and pushed gingerly on them. They scarcely moved. "That ain't so easy," she said.

"Because the sheep's pushing against you," said Enoch. "With the calf that time Clark and Lizzie really had to shove at it."

"Okay," said Rita, "I'm pushing harder. But it's not going. I'm afraid I'll hurt it, break the legs or something. Let me try turning the head without it."

For a few moments there was silence while she worked.

"Can't get it," she said at last. "Can't get a hold on it. It's wedged too tight."

"The book says you might have to hook your thumb and finger in the jaw," said Gyp. "To get a better grip."

"Gyp, come sit here and hold the sheep," said Enoch. "I'm going to help Rita." So Gyp came and took Enoch's place, and Enoch went around behind. Mercy shifted and let him kneel beside Rita.

"What are you going to do?" said Mercy.

"Push it in," said Enoch, taking hold of the two little legs.

"Okay, Enoch," said Rita. "We're going to get it this time. Ready?"

"Let's go," said Enoch, and he began pushing in on the legs.

"Careful, Enoch," whispered Mercy.

"It's okay," said Enoch. "We're getting it now."

"Yeah, push, Enoch," said Rita. "It's working. I can move the head a little now. Give me just a little more room. Yeah, there. Okay. I'm getting it. Yeah, there. I got it. I got it. Oh, praise be. We got it."

Enoch sat back and Rita slowly pulled out her hand, the nose of the lamb following her fingers.

"Here it comes," said Mercy, excited, the light jiggling.

"Hold still with the light," said Enoch, and then he

97

reached back and took it himself. The nose was showing now, but that was all. It had stopped.

"Oh, no," whispered Mercy.

Then the ewe gave a heave and out came the head and shoulders.

"Come on, sheep," murmured Rita, and the ewe lay still for a moment and then heaved again, and the lamb was born.

"Oh, good," Mercy said softly. "There it is. What a nice lamb. And look, it's breathing. Oh, mama sheep, you did good."

"You did good, too," Enoch said to Rita, looking at her and then feeling the numbness for the first time that night, the flustered bumbling welling up in him.

"You, too," said Rita. "All three of you. We all did good. But what now? Do we clean it off?"

"See first if she will," said Enoch, not looking at Rita, fighting to keep his mind off her, to keep it clear. He picked up the lamb and carried it around to the ewe, who sniffed it and began to lick it and then struggled to her feet and stood washing it, patiently licking, as if there was nothing new about it. Enoch watched them, feeling proud. Then Rita was beside him, close beside him, and she was laying a hand on his back.

"You don't know how glad I am you were here," she said quietly. "I don't think I would have even tried it otherwise." She paused, a long pause, her hand still on his back. "You know, Enoch," she said, and her voice was soft in his ear, "you don't belong in Raleigh. You belong here on Kettle Creek. You really do. I hope you won't go away."

Maybe I won't, he wanted to say, but with her hand on his back he could not utter a word.

So maybe now he would not go. Maybe now that she saw him differently, now that he was no longer a child to her, maybe now was not the time to leave. She said that she wanted him to stay. She said it with her hand on his back. That lovely hand. He could still feel it. He always would. He could not remember anymore why he had wanted to go. He could only remember her hand and her voice. And if those two things, that hand and that voice, were the promise that he hoped for, then he would be a fool to walk away from it. Perhaps to her, free and independent as she was, perhaps to her the eleven years between them were nothing. Perhaps the hand and the voice had promised that, that the eleven years would be nothing now. He wanted to know if that was so, because if it was, he would not go to Raleigh. He would stay and be with Rita.

So the following day he looked for her, hoping he would run into her while walking on the dirt road or checking on the lamb in the pasture or killing time at B&B's. But he only saw her once and that from a distance when he heard her truck coming down the valley and he went out on the porch and waved as she drove by without stopping, without even slowing down. That was when he walked to B&B's, thinking she was headed there, but she was not. When she returned that evening, he was in the barn, milking, and he heard the truck and hoped to hear it pull in the driveway, but it went on by and up the valley. Then Clark and Lizzie came home from the festival, and as Mercy bubbled on to them about the lamb, it all began to seem unreal, as if he had only dreamed it, especially the part at the end, the hand on his back and the voice.

But lying in bed that night it came back to him, clear and

vivid and exciting. And he resolved that tomorrow he would go to her house, not wait for a chance meeting but go directly to her and find out.

Rita was in the garden when the bucket of rocks rattled in her front yard. She was on her knees beside the carrots, thinning them, pulling up young plants with sweet tender roots two inches long and dropping them in the basket beside her. She worked on a few minutes longer, then got to her feet and picked up the basket and walked into the cool shade of her front yard and stood looking toward the path, waiting for whoever it was to come around the spur of the hill. When she saw it was Enoch, it surprised her. He was not a customary visitor, not like the younger children. If he came, it was usually to deliver a message of some sort.

He waved, then came on up the path without looking at her, keeping his eyes on the ground ahead of him until he was close enough to speak. Then he looked up at her, meeting her eyes and her smile, and said, "So how's it going?"

"Pretty good," she said. "How about you?"

"All right," he said. Then his eyes wavered and flickered down and away and looked beyond her, off to one side. She could feel his unease, and she spoke quickly to smooth it for him, asking him if he had stopped to see the lamb on his way.

His face relaxed and his eyes steadied and came back to her. "It's a fine-looking lamb," he said. "Pretty as can be."

"The ewe seems to have come through all right," she said.

"She looks good," said Enoch. "Melinda says they're both healthy. In good shape."

"I guess we done good," said Rita.

"Sure did," he said, and then came a pause in which he seemed about to say something else. But his eyes lost their hold and looked away. She was wondering now why he had come. There seemed to be no message to be given, no outward purpose. She felt sorry for him, standing there so awkwardly.

"I've been thinning carrots," she said, raising the basket to show him.

"Is there more to do?" he said. "I'll help."

"I can finish it later," she said. "Thanks anyway."

"No, I'll help you. I'd like to. Come show me where to start." And he was already heading for the garden, so she followed him, thinking now that she might have an idea of why he had come.

"Here," she said, directing him to the carrot row.

"I'll start down here," he said, and already he was at the end of the row, kneeling down and getting to work. She stood for a moment and watched him, wondering what to do about him, and then, not deciding, she started in at the opposite end of the row. Enoch seemed content just to be there, working quietly. He began to hum a tune and then to sing softly. The distance between them gradually narrowed and after a while, when they were close enough for easy conversation, he stopped singing. But he did not say anything.

So Rita said, "What are you going to do with yourself now that school is out?"

"Work, mainly," he said. "I'm going to help Stuart sucker that field of tomatoes. Starting next week. He said you might be working for him, too."

"I might," said Rita. "I need the money."

"I'm also going to do some haying," said Enoch.

101

"Who for?"

"For whoever'll hire me. And at home, of course, but I don't get paid for that."

"Sounds like you'll be busy."

"Yeah, and Clark says we're going to be doing some work on the barn, replacing some of the siding and stuff like that. And Mountain Man wants me and Gyp to go to Asheville with him on flea market days like we did last summer. So I'd say there's plenty to do." He sat back on his heels and studied the carrot he had just pulled up, turned it in his fingers and wiped all the dirt from it. "But, you know," he said slowly, "there's not so much that I couldn't come up here and help you with any work you might need done. And I don't mean for pay. I'd just like to come up and . . . Well, it's like you said. Maybe I shouldn't go to Raleigh. Maybe I should just stay here and come up and help you do things. I mean, things you might need help with. If you want me to." He had forgotten about thinning the carrots now, was putting everything into his words; but she was going along with her work as if what he was giving her was idle conversation and nothing more. And yet she knew. She heard him and sensed what lay behind the words and knew she must deal with it.

"I don't really need any help," she said, not looking up. "When Bo was here he helped me with everything I needed. There's nothing now I can't manage by myself."

"But things go faster with two people," said Enoch. "Look at these carrots. We're almost done."

"But I could have done it alone," said Rita, and still she was pulling carrots as if nothing that mattered was being said. "In fact, I'd usually rather work alone. I like the tranquillity of it. I don't mean to say I don't appreciate you helping me out here, but generally speaking, I like the solitude. Most of the time I'd rather not have any help." And still she was thinning carrots, working away as if none of it had meaning.

"I see," Enoch said quietly, and he went back to work. They were almost finished, and he worked more quickly than before, not talking now and not humming or singing, but almost hurrying along, as if he wanted to get through with the job and go home. As soon as the last carrot was pulled, he was on his feet.

"Guess I'll be going," he said.

"All right," she said. She wanted to say something more, something nice, but could think of nothing he might not misconstrue, for she was sure now that she knew why he had come and he must not come back for it again. So she only said, "Good-by now." And as he walked away she did not even stand and watch him go, but turned and went into her house because he would have known if she had stood and watched, and even in that he might have found a ray of hope.

So now Enoch knew. The hand and the voice had meant nothing. He had been a fool. She had made it clear to him, and now he knew. He was humiliated and in anguish, but at least he knew, and that was better than keeping on a fool. Now he must get away from her, far away, as quickly as possible. And so his feet walked swiftly down the path, his face and neck hot at first with embarrassment but cooler as he reached the rutted driveway. He went down it with the same fast, long-legged stride, on past the Nashes' to the dirt road and then along the road past Mountain Man's house and past the Harrimans', and on toward his own house, until he saw Gyp ahead and slowed his pace and gathered his composure.

Gyp was walking up from the mailboxes that were down at the paved road, and when he saw Enoch he waved something he had in his hand. As the distance between them narrowed, Enoch could see it was a book, and when they came within speaking range, Gyp held it up and said, "Daddy's latest, hot off the press. *The Reactor Factor.*" He had the rest of the mail and the brown envelope the book had come in tucked under one arm.

Enoch made an effort to respond normally. "Is this Roosevelt Washington or Jasmina DeBayou?" he asked, reaching for the book.

"This is one of Roosevelt's cases," said Gyp. "Daddy let me read the manuscript. The gist of it is that the Secretary of Energy gets assassinated by the greedy forces of international capitalism because he's about to go public against nuclear power. Pretty good, huh?"

"It's plausible," said Enoch.

"Of course, the murder's made to look like a boating accident, but Roosevelt figures it out and cracks the case. As usual."

"Sounds good," said Enoch, thumbing through the book, trying to hide his lack of interest, the hollowness of his feelings.

"You know," said Gyp, "Roosevelt's always going after the greedy forces of international capitalism in these books. Seems like the greedy forces wouldn't put up with a detective like that for very long. Seems like they'd be trying to wipe him out."

104

"You ought to talk to Morgan about it," said Enoch.

"He could write a book just about that," said Gyp. "The greedy forces taking aim at Roosevelt. Maybe Jasmina De-Bayou could come in and save him."

Enoch's laugh was short and flat.

Gyp looked at him. "You doing all right?" he asked.

Enoch shrugged. "Yeah, I'm all right. Maybe dreading a little bit going home, is all. I'm going to make the big announcement tonight. The final decision."

"You're going to go to Raleigh, huh?"

"Yep."

"Well, that's a kick in the ass," said Gyp, and he looked down at the ground and pushed at a stone with his foot. "A real kick in the ass."

"Well . . ." said Enoch, and he looked down, too, concentrating on the same rock. "That's the way it is."

"Phew," Gyp said quietly, shaking his head. "I'd hate to be in your house tonight. Mercy's going to cry for sure. And Clark's going to raise holy hell. And Lizzie, I don't know what she'll do."

"She'll be cool like she always is," said Enoch. "And the rest of them will, too, after a while."

"I reckon they'll have to," said Gyp. "What made you decide so all of a sudden?"

"Not so all of a sudden," said Enoch. "I was always planning to go, you know that. But they said I had to wait for summer to say so. So now it's summer."

"Yeah, but why today?" said Gyp. "All of a sudden like this?"

"No particular reason," said Enoch, and he looked out across the valley. For a time he was silent. Then he said, "Guess I'd better be getting on home."

"Okay," said Gyp. "But it was something that made you decide. You don't have to tell me. I just wish it hadn't happened, is all."

Enoch looked at him for a long moment. "I wish you were coming to Raleigh, too," he said.

Gyp shook his head. "Not me." He gave the rock a hard kick. "I guess I'll see you later." He turned and began walking down the road toward his house.

"Tell Morgan I said the book looks good," said Enoch.

"I'll do that," Gyp said over his shoulder.

"And tell him your idea for a new story."

"Sure," said Gyp. "I'll do that too."

Enoch stood for a moment longer, watching him. Then he turned away and headed home.

SEVEN

Enoch insisted on doing all the milking on his last night at home. Everything was ready for him to go. His trunk was packed, his bus ticket was in his wallet, his mother's saved up money was spent on new clothes for him, his father's man-to-man talk was delivered—that long serious talk about drugs and girls and reckless driving; his aunt and uncle and cousins were expecting him, had a room prepared for him, had him registered for school; and his going away party was starting at the Harrimans'. But still Enoch went to the barn and did all the milking himself. He did not want Clark to have to do any of it, or Lizzie, or Mercy. He was pulling out on them. He saw it that way now. He was leaving the three of them with more work to do, his work, and he did not feel good about it. The milking was a kind of penance, though a feeble one. When he had finished it, he did not feel any better.

He walked alone to his farewell party, for he had insisted, in his penance, that the others go ahead without him. He took the old path through the pasture, and as he walked along, he tried to savor it, to experience it as the last time, as something to store up and keep with him in his absence. But he could not feel it that way. It seemed like just another August evening with the sun dropping down behind Brokeleg Mountain and the valley filling with soft, heat-chasing shadow. When he came to Kettle Creek under the green drooping trees, he stopped on the bank and squatted down and put his hand into the water and felt its coolness and its life. And there for an instant he had what he was seeking, a sense of leavetaking, an awareness that this was the last time and tomorrow all would be different. But then his sense of it was gone, and he could not bring it back again.

He went on across the creek and over the fence into the Harrimans' pasture and up to the house, to the side yard where the grown-ups were playing softball in the fading light while down near the barn the children played hide-and-seek.

Gladys was at bat in the ball game—she was thirteen, just old enough to be a grown-up when it came to sports. Mountain Man was leading off from first base, looking as if he might steal second. Melinda was pitching. Geneen was the first baseman, Clark was playing second, and Gyp was playing third. Betty was the shortstop, and Rita, Bud, and D. J. were in the outfield. Stuart was catcher. The rest of the other team were scattered around behind home plate, rooting for Gladys, waiting for their turns at bat.

Mr. and Mrs. Iverson were on the sidelines, and so were two of the Flint Creek people, and Wanda, who was nursing her new baby, and Bill Nash, who was keeping an eye on Dee and Dum and Bubba. The little ones were absorbed in the game, especially Bubba, whose attention was riveted on his sister at home plate. Enoch went over and sat beside them.

"Who's winning?" he asked.

"Gladys is," said Dum, getting up from the grass and coming over and dropping into Enoch's lap. Enoch put an arm around him.

"Is that right, Bubba?" said Enoch, leaning over toward Bubba. "Is your sister winning?"

Bubba smiled and nodded, turning his face shyly away.

"Gyp is, too," said Dee.

"But they're not on the same team," said Enoch. "Only one of them can be winning."

"Gladys is," Bubba said softly.

Bill shook his head and laughed. "The other team is," he said. "Six to four."

"Come on, Gladys!" Enoch called. "Even it up!" She looked around and grinned. Then she turned back and Melinda pitched the ball. Gladys swung and hit a pop fly that Clark should have had, but he missed it in the deepening twilight, and Mountain Man got to second and Gladys was safe on first.

"Way to go, Gladys!" yelled Enoch.

"Way to go!" Dee and Dum echoed.

Bubba grinned. "Home run," he said.

"No," said Enoch. "With a home run you go to all the bases."

"Gyp hit a home run," said Dee.

"Three home runs," said Dum.

"So did my mama," said Dee. "She hit four."

109

"She hit a no-hitter," said Dum.

Enoch laughed. "Y'all don't know what you're talking about."

"They haven't told you a true thing yet," said Bill.

"You don't hit no-hitters," Enoch said to Dum. "You pitch them."

"My mama's pitching," said Dum. "That's what she's doing right now."

"I know," said Enoch. "But she's not pitching a no-hitter because people are hitting the ball. In a no-hitter, nobody gets a hit."

"But Gladys hit a home run," said Dee.

"Not a home run," said Enoch. "Just a hit."

"A base hit," Bubba said softly.

"Hey, that's right, Bubba," said Enoch, reaching over and messing up his hair. Bubba laughed and ducked his head. Then Enoch had it again, the sense of leavetaking, and he paused for a moment with his hand on Bubba's head, and it felt like sorrow. But then it was gone, like before, and this was just another late summer evening with another ball game ending before it was over because it was getting too dark to see the ball.

Dinner was a pot-luck feast of country ham and fried chicken and fresh vegetables and crisp salads and fruit pies, everything homegrown and delicious. Enoch piled his plate full and went out to sit in the yard with Gyp and Gladys and Mountain Man. When Lizzie came to join them, they moved back to make the circle larger, and when Morgan came, they moved again.

"Anybody else comes, they can start another circle," said Mountain Man. But Billy Boy came and they moved over far enough to let him in.

"You're not going to get food like this in Raleigh," Morgan said to Enoch.

Enoch shrugged. "Maybe not."

"I don't know," said Mountain Man. "There are some city folks that've taken to growing vegetables these days."

"Not my brother-in-law," said Lizzie. "He and Linda are too avant-garde for anything like that. They believe in microwave ovens and space food."

"They're not that bad," said Enoch.

"Well, that ain't avant-garde, anyway," said Mountain Man.

"What's avant-garde mean?" said Billy Boy.

"It means being ahead of folks on things," said Mountain Man. "Leading the pack. Being the first one into the future. But it ain't avant-garde if you're heading down a blind alley."

"What do you mean?" said Gladys.

"Well, there's two schools of thought on the future," said Mountain Man. "One is the microwave-oven-and-space-food school. Those are folks that think we'll all be living in chrome houses in the future and ordering our groceries by home computer. They got it all figured out. They'll tell you that we'll have farms orbiting in space someday. Now ain't that wonderful? No weather problems. Just push a button, and it rains. Push another button, the sun comes out."

Billy Boy laughed and Mountain Man glanced at him appreciatively.

"Yeah, but what's the future really going to be like?" said Gyp.

"Like this," said Mountain Man, sweeping his fork around. "Like us. The energy and resources are all going to dwindle down. Folks won't be able to have so much stuff

111

anymore. And what they'll find out is, they don't need it after all. It wasn't even making them happy. All they need is a house, not too big. They need some fuel, and they need it to be something renewable like wood or sun or wind so the scarcity of it don't send them to the poorhouse. They need good nonchemical food so they don't keep getting cancer. And they need to buy it from somebody growing it nearby because there ain't going to be the gas anymore to truck it in from California. That means eating things in season, and people won't like the notion of that at first, but once they try it, they'll like it. It peaks life up to have it come round in seasons."

"They need jobs," said Morgan.

"Yep, and there'll be a lot more of those in the future. The less fuel we have to power all this technology, the more we'll need human labor. And that don't have to be a bad thing, not if we're organized and share the load."

"But we're not so organized around here," said Lizzie.

"Maybe not as much as we'll need to be. Right now there ain't that many of us and there's still enough looseness in things that we can all kind of slop around and still get by. But I tell you true, this is a whole lot closer to where everybody's going than that space farm is."

"I agree with that," said Lizzie, and Morgan nodded his head.

"Looks like you're heading out the wrong way, Enoch," said Gyp.

"No, I ain't saying that," said Mountain Man. "Maybe Enoch needs to go. Because the future's not here yet. He says he don't want to be ignorant about the world, and I don't blame him for that."

Enoch twiddled his fork along his empty plate, not saying anything. Morgan, sitting beside him, put a hand on his shoulder and shook it gently.

"But we're going to miss you," he said. "Every day that goes by, we'll miss you."

"We sure will, Enoch," said Gladys.

"I'll miss y'all, too," Enoch said, looking up, making his voice sound more cheerful than he felt.

"You'll especially miss my inspiring lectures, I reckon," said Mountain Man.

Enoch smiled. "Especially those."

"You will miss them, Enoch," said Lizzie, her voice almost stern. Enoch glanced at her and saw her eyes glistening.

"I know," he said softly.

"Well, I'm going to get some dessert," said Billy Boy, getting to his feet.

Enoch got up and followed after him. "That's a pretty good idea."

It felt like the last night now. Leavetaking was with him, weighing on him. Billy Boy ran ahead, but Enoch walked slowly, then stopped altogether, absorbed in the moment, seeing everything with a startling clarity, feeling it intensely—the warmth of the night and the voices in it, the closeness and familiarity. It seemed wonderful to him. The laughter in the yard. The strum of his father's guitar on the porch. It was like when they lived in the barn, that early time, grown-ups all around, talking, singing low, and he and Gyp falling asleep in the midst of them.

And suddenly he did not want to go away. He was seeing it now, seeing it clearly, and he did not want to leave it.

113

Was this how Clark could always see it? And Mercy and Gyp? They had tried to tell him. Why had he not seen it before? Why only now when it was too late, too late to back out after all he had said and done, after all that had happened? It had come too far.

"I thought you were going for dessert," said Gyp, coming up behind him.

"I am," said Enoch.

"Then come on. We'll miss Brandy's apple pie."

"Wouldn't want to do that," said Enoch, and he led the way onto the porch and through the house to the kitchen. Most of the kids were there waiting for everyone to have firsts on desserts so they could pounce on seconds. Rita was there, too, sitting on a stool, leaning back on her elbows against a counter, talking to Bill and Melinda and Betty.

"Here's our sojourner," she said when Enoch came in.

"Tanking up on pie," said Enoch. "One last time." He went to the table and concentrated on serving up the pie, keeping his eyes off Rita. Things had eased between them after working together in Stuart's tomato field, but still for Enoch there was the problem of her femaleness. It was basic. He could not rid himself of it. He did not even want to.

"You ought to save yourself out a piece of that pie to take with you on the bus," said Betty.

"Nah. Too messy," said Enoch.

"What time's the bus going to leave?" Effie asked. "Early?"

"Pretty early," he said. "Eight fifteen. Got to get up at six, I guess."

"Yeah, you'll have to do the milking first, won't you?" said Billy Boy.

114

"No, I think Lizzie and Mercy are going to do that. They'll be staying home. Clark's the only one taking me to Fairmont."

"Oh, let's not talk about it," said Mercy, sadness catching at her voice. "Let's have some music or something."

"Go find Brandy," said Bill. "That's her department."

"She's on the porch," said Gyp. "She's still eating."

"Try Mountain Man, then," said Melinda. "He'd probably come play you a tune."

"Did I hear my name?" said Mountain Man, coming into the room.

"You did," said Betty. "Miss Mercy wants some music. Something cheerful."

"Something cheerful, is it?" he said, taking his harmonica from his pocket. "Enoch, dish me up a piece of that pie and hide it away up there on the refrigerator. Don't none of you kids get it, either."

"We won't," said the children, shaking their heads.

"We won't, we promise," Dum said after the others. "Dee won't either."

"I won't," Dee said solemnly.

Mountain Man laughed. "I ain't too worried," he said, and he put the harmonica to his lips, cupping his hands around it. He ran up and down it a couple of times, warming up.

Enoch set away a piece of pie for Mountain Man and then took his own plate and went over and sat down beside Mercy. She linked her arm into his, and he squeezed it against his side and held it there, even though her clapping to the music made it hard for him to eat. Mountain Man was playing "Mountain Dew," and the children were singing along:

They call it that good old mountain dew,
And them that refuse it are few.
  (Mighty few!)
You can go round the bend,
But you'll come back again
For that good old mountain dew.

The party did not break up until midnight. The small children were carried home asleep. Enoch walked home with his mother and father and sister, the sliver of new moon barely lighting their way down the Harrimans' driveway to the dirt road. They walked in silence. Leavetaking was tight in Enoch's throat. On his arms and chest he still felt the hugs—tight, warm, awkward hugs—and in his mind the song turned and turned, the last song of the evening, sung without instruments . . . *It's a gift to be simple, it's a gift to be free.* . . . He wanted to speak to Clark, to tell him that he had changed his mind. He wanted to tell him that he did not want to go away anymore . . . *it's a gift to come down where we ought to be.* . . . But it was too late even to say so, too late to do anything except follow the plan, get on the bus, go to Raleigh and try to like it there . . . *and when we find ourselves in the place just right.* . . .

They turned off the road into their driveway, and as they started up it, Enoch sighed—a deep, wearisome, trembling sigh. Clark reached out and put an arm around his shoulders, and Enoch, drawing close to his father, felt like crying.

116

EIGHT

Craig leaned toward Enoch and said something. Enoch could see his cousin's mouth moving and hear snatches of his voice as it swirled into the pulsating din of the discotheque.

"What?" Enoch shouted, leaning closer.

Craig motioned toward the door. Enoch nodded and they all three got up, Craig and Enoch following Jay along the edge of the dance floor, detouring around tables, dodging stray dancers and stumbling drunks. The boys themselves were a little drunk, but they walked straight enough as they broke free of the crowd and strolled out past the cashier who earlier in the evening had checked their IDs and collected their money. Enoch and Craig both had acceptable IDs. Jay knew how to arrange such things. Jay's own card was legitimate. He really was eighteen.

They followed Jay out into the warm September night.

"As I was saying," said Craig when the door had swung shut behind them. "How about a smoke break?"

"Sure," said Enoch, feeling the lightness in his head. How much beer had he had? Two pitchers for the three of them? No, three. They had ordered one more. "Where do we do it?" he said. "In the car?"

"No," said Jay. "They watch the parking lot."

"We drive around," said Craig. "That's the safest way."

Again Jay led them as they zigzagged among the parked cars. He took keys from his pocket and unlocked the door on the passenger side of Craig's car and got in. Craig unlocked the driver's side and opened the door, then stood out of the way for Enoch. Pulling the seat forward, Enoch crawled into the back and settled down comfortably.

"God, that was dull," said Craig as he got in and started the engine. "I've never seen so many unfriendly girls."

"Unfriendly to you, maybe," said Jay.

"Yeah, you did all right. But me and Enoch didn't do a thing. Did we, Enoch?"

"Not nothing," said Enoch.

"They all had somebody," said Craig, backing the car out. "I couldn't see getting a broken nose asking for a dance that wasn't going to take me anywhere."

"You got to know how to pick them," said Jay.

"We could have picked a better place," said Craig, pulling out of the parking lot into the traffic. "A place with friendlier girls."

"That's only in your dreams," said Jay. He reached beneath the dashboard and brought out a marijuana cigarette. "Left," he said, and Craig put on his blinker and made a left turn. Jay held the joint in his hand, not lighting up. "So how do you like it here, Enoch?" he said, tilting up his head to throw his voice to the back.

118

"Great," said Enoch. "I'm having a fine time." He sat forward and leaned his arms on the backs of the two bucket seats. He was feeling the beer. "You know," he said, "I like it better than I thought I would. I've hardly thought about home in the two weeks I've been here. I guess I've been having too much fun."

"We'll take you to Wonderland tonight," said Jay.

"What's that?" said Enoch.

"A parking lot where lots of us hang out," said Craig. "Wonderland Shopping Center. Gets lively about this time of night."

"Usually there's some unattached girls," said Jay. "And plenty of booze. Hunch punch is our specialty."

"Hunch punch?" laughed Enoch.

"Fruit punch and straight grain. Girls get drunk before they know it. Go right down for you."

"Sounds good," said Enoch.

"Better than that disco," said Craig. "I promise you."

"Left," said Jay, and Craig braked and turned left again. They were on a residential street now and Jay took matches from his shirt pocket. "Watch your speed," he said, and Craig slowed a little. Jay lit up the joint, lingered over it, and then, almost reluctantly, passed it around. When it was gone, Jay directed Craig back to a thoroughfare and Craig headed on toward Wonderland. Enoch settled lengthwise in the back seat and watched the lights go by.

"When do you get your license back, Jay?" he said.

"Five years," said Jay. "Well, four and a half now. It's been six months since they took it."

"He was framed," said Craig.

"Yeah, goddamn framed," said Jay. "By a cop. A cop with a grudge. You get a cop testifying against you and you don't stand a prayer."

119

"Why'd he have a grudge?" said Enoch.

"Damned if I know," said Jay. "Just decided he didn't like me. Hassled me for years every chance he got. Then he's the one turns up at the wreck. Says I was drunk. Harasses me about it, right there on the spot. Goes on and on with it. As if I didn't already feel bad enough about my buddy lying there dead. I wasn't drunk. Not that drunk, anyway."

"Bum rap," said Enoch, feeling the marijuana, perceiving through it a momentousness in Jay's account, a blatancy in the injustice.

"As if Bobby being dead wasn't enough suffering for me," Jay complained, "they got to take away my wheels, too."

"The bastards," Enoch muttered.

"If it wasn't for Craig, here, I'd be in rough shape. But old Craig, he's a good-un. Takes me where I need to go."

Craig seemed pleased, straightening his shoulders. "You'd do the same for me," he said.

"Any time you need me, hoss, I'll be there," Jay said. "Any time."

They drifted into silence. Enoch watched the street, the sparse traffic in the four lanes, the street lights going by one after another, keeping away the darkness. He watched the shops slide past, closed but dimly lit inside, shuttered, some of them, with steel mesh. And now and then a gas station floated by, flooded with lights, watched over by a cashier in a glass booth.

Craig slowed for a left turn and Enoch sat forward, leaning up against the seat backs, peering out the front to see where they were going.

"This is Wonderland," said Craig as he pulled into the huge parking lot, empty except for the cars parked at one end around an all-night fast food restaurant. Craig headed for the restaurant, cutting diagonally across the lot.

"The police keep an eye on this place," Jay said. "The rule is, don't do anything stupid. Assume you're being watched."

Craig pulled in among the other parked cars. There were people in most of them. Jay got out and climbed in the next car. Craig rolled down his window and exchanged a few words with the people beside him. Enoch sat back and watched. In a few minutes Jay came back eating a piece of pizza.

"Not much happening," he said. The smell of the pizza filled the car.

"I was thinking Judy might be here," said Craig. "She said she might."

"She is," said Jay. "In Tina's car."

"Well, that's something," said Craig, brightening.

Jay shrugged. "Bart's got the booze in his car if you want some."

"Do they sell pizza here?" asked Enoch.

Jay shook his head. "Just hamburgers. This came from somewhere else." He took another bite and Enoch looked away, too hungry to watch.

"I guess I'll wander over and talk to Judy," said Craig.

"I'm going to get a hamburger," said Enoch. Craig got out and Enoch unfolded after him. "Anybody else want anything?" he said.

"You can get me a Coke," said Craig. "Something to put a little booze in."

"Jay?" said Enoch, looking back into the car.

"Nah," said Jay, putting the last bit of pizza in his mouth.

When Enoch got back, the car was empty. He set Craig's drink on the floor in the front and climbed into his place in the back. He had finished his hamburger and was settling back sleepily when Craig returned.

"Hey, Enoch," said Craig, opening the door and pulling the seat forward. "Here's somebody I want you to meet." And suddenly there was a girl coming into the back. Enoch gathered himself together.

"I'm Florrie," she said, sitting down beside him.

"Nice to meet you," said Enoch.

"You're the cousin we've been hearing about," she said.

"I guess so," said Enoch. Another girl was getting into the car, sliding across the driver's seat to the passenger side.

"This is Judy," said Craig, getting in after her. "My cousin Enoch," he added, making a brief motion with his hand toward Enoch.

"Hi, Enoch," said Judy.

"Hi," said Enoch, beginning to feel stupid. He glanced at Florrie. Was he supposed to do anything with her? Had she been drinking hunch punch? She was settling into the corner, tucking back her feet with her knees pointed toward him. No way to get close to her like that. He looked at her and she smiled, a friendly enough smile but with a definite coolness. Either she had not been drinking hunch punch or she was immune to it.

They sat and talked, the four of them, for a long time, or at least it seemed a long time to Enoch. Mostly they talked about people he had never heard of. He was getting sleepy and may even have dozed off, he was not sure. All he knew was that Jay was suddenly leaning in at Craig's window telling them that Tina was taking Jay home and would Craig take the other girls home? Enoch came fully awake at

122

the thought of what might be required of him between Wonderland and Florrie's home.

Florrie, however, required nothing of him, not even a walk to her door. "Don't bother," she said as he made a move to follow her from the car. Once out, she leaned down to Craig's window and looked back in at Enoch. "Nice meeting you," she said. Then she patted Craig's shoulder. "Be good," she told him, and she turned and walked up the flagstone walk. Enoch watched her go, wondering if there was anything he could have done to have made it a more successful encounter.

Craig was obviously more practiced. And he did know Judy better. But even so, he did not get very far. When they stopped at Judy's house, there were a few awkward moments while he and Judy groped in the front seat. Enoch tried not to pay attention, though there was not much else to do. He looked down at his hands and out the window and back at his hands again. He was relieved when Judy said she had to go in. While Craig went with her to the door, Enoch moved up to the front seat and settled down for a long wait. But in a few moments Craig was back.

"Where to now?" Craig said, and Enoch was surprised at his high spirits. He had supposed that by Craig's standards the night had been a washout.

"I'd love to have a pizza," said Enoch. "Can we get one this late?"

"Are you kidding?" said Craig. "In this town we can get anything."

Enoch woke up by degrees. The telephone had been ringing. He opened his eyes once and closed them again, dozing.

"Mama!" Lisa's voice brought him back. "Telephone!" Enoch blinked opened his eyes again and looked over at the curtained window. Full daylight. It was late. He reached for his watch on the nightstand. Ten thirty. Almost noon. But so what? No cows to milk. No barn chores. Jesus, what luxury.

He stretched and folded his hands behind his head and looked lazily around the room at the posters of rock stars and television sex queens and the stereo—his own stereo. He still could not get over that: a stereo for every member of the family. His had belonged to Lisa until she got a new one last month for her fourteenth birthday. All these stereos, but they spent their time watching television. Ned and Linda had a television in their bedroom. Another one, in the den, was never off. He could hear it now. Saturday morning cartoons. That was the one thing he was having trouble with. For the last two Saturdays he had tried to watch them. Craig and Lisa stayed glued to the set. For them Saturday morning *was* cartoons, nothing else. Maybe you had to be raised on it.

He pushed back the covers and got up, digging his toes into the soft carpet. How nice it was, even after three weeks, to walk barefoot to the bathroom and have his feet stay clean and warm. How nice to have a bathroom to walk to. One with a john, that is. No walking out through the dew or frost. Everything warm and cozy and convenient. And the shower. No solar-heated tank that would not heat up on a rainy day. A hot shower anytime, day or night, rain or shine. And light. Let there be light in the bathroom. Just flip the switch.

He got into the shower and stayed there a long time, letting the hot water beat against his neck and shoulders. He did not feel too bad, considering the night he had had, another hard-charging one with Craig and Jay. Those two could sure enough pack away the beer. He had given up trying to keep up with them. Smoking, too. He just did not like the way he felt when he smoked that much pot. He liked to keep more in touch with himself than that.

Out of the shower and into his jeans. Now for his two big responsibilities of the day—brushing his teeth and making his bed. That was all he had to do. Nothing more. Except show up for meals. A king could not have it any better. Except a king would not have to make his bed. There was still something left to aim for.

Enoch padded down to the kitchen in his stocking feet. He was spending a lot of time these days in his socks. With carpet everywhere there was no need for shoes, not unless he was going outside, and no need to go outside unless he was going somewhere. He looked in the den. Craig was up, watching cartoons with Lisa. Enoch stood in the doorway and watched the set. Too dumb. He could not watch them again this morning. Anyway, he needed something to eat.

In the kitchen he found doughnuts. What would Lizzie say? She would say it was awful. Then she would say: At least pick out the doughnut with the least sugar glumped on it, and drink a glass of milk for some protein, and can you find some fruit or something?

Enoch poured himself a large glass of milk, picked out two relatively colorless doughnuts, and rummaged in the refrigerator until he found an overripe apple, bruised and sorry-looking. He peeled it, throwing away the skin with its invisible residue of chemical sprays. How's that, Lizzie? But she did not answer. And again, as in the three weeks since he had come, he was vaguely puzzled that he was so seldom visited by images from home.

He found the morning newspaper and took it and his

125

breakfast to the dining-room table. The door to Ned's study was partly closed, and he could hear Linda's voice behind it. They called it Ned's study, but it was more like the telephone room. Enoch folded the front section of the paper in half and propped it against the sugar bowl. Africa again. Where the resources are.

". . . Ned's nephew," he heard Linda say. He looked up from the paper and listened. "No, I wouldn't say that," said Linda. "Three are no worse than two. Not so far, anyway." Then a pause. "Well, Ned feels he owes the boy something. His only nephew, and here his brother has gone and raised him like a primitive. None of the advantages. Not even a real school. Not even electricity, for god's sake." A short pause. "That's the one. Clark. The family hippie." Another pause, longer. "Well, actually, Marie, he's a very good boy. We hope he'll have a settling influence on Craig." Pause. "Oh, nothing really. Craig's a good boy. No trouble. But he is a senior now, you know. It gets harder and harder to keep the reins tight. Damned hard, if you want to know the truth. Especially when he's running around with this older boy already out of school." Pause. "No, Jay's a good boy. It's just that he's older."

It bothered Enoch the way she had talked about his father. He gathered up his unfinished breakfast, abandoned the paper, and went into the den to watch cartoons.

Enoch was singing in the back seat of the car, singing louder and louder until Lisa turned around and looked at him.

"How can you do it?" she said. "How can you be so happy on a Monday morning?"

"School," he said. "I love it."

Craig groaned.

"You'll get tired of it," said Lisa. "Won't he, Craig?"

"He ought to be already," said Craig. "Four weeks ought to take the shine off it for anybody."

"Not me," said Enoch. "I love it."

"How come?" said Lisa. "Name one good thing about it."

"The people," said Enoch. "All the people. There's so much that can happen with that many people."

"Yeah, you could be trampled to death," said Craig.

"No, good things," said Enoch.

"Like what?" said Lisa.

"Like friends. Like girl friends. Like interesting things that could happen between classes. In classes. Like, I don't know. Like lots of things."

"You call a fight a good thing?" said Craig. "That's all I ever see happen between classes."

Enoch did not say anything.

"Name something good you've seen," said Craig.

"Friends together," said Enoch.

"But that's nothing," said Lisa. "Nothing happens."

"But something could," said Enoch. "With all those people, you never know. Here we are going to school thinking it's going to be a regular day, but who knows, something wonderful might happen to you or to Craig or to me."

"Christ," said Craig. "What gibberish."

"Yeah, that's too unreal, Enoch," said Lisa. "Name something real you like about school."

"Classes," said Enoch. "Lunch. Pep rallies. Clubs. The whole bit. I like it all."

127

"Well, it's true, some of it's not so bad," said Lisa.

"That's because you're just a freshman," Craig said to her. "Take it from me. It's all bad."

"Maybe classes aren't so good," said Lisa. "But I like pep rallies."

"I like classes," said Enoch.

"You're crazy," said Craig. "How about changing the subject to something less disgusting."

"I even like textbooks," said Enoch.

"Okay. Enough," said Craig.

"Didn't you have textbooks at your school back home?" said Lisa.

"Sure we did," said Enoch. "But I like there being thirty other people with the same book. I don't know why."

"Nobody learns anything," said Craig. "Everybody cheats."

Enoch did not say anything. He knew about the cheating. He had seen it. Craig cheated and made no secret of it. Maybe Lisa cheated, too. It was the thing about school he could not understand. With such a fine school, why did they all want to cheat?

The morning sun was warming up the car. They were only a few blocks from school now. They stopped at an intersection and Enoch rolled down his window. A warm feeling washed over him, something deep and soul-filling, like coffee brewing on a wood stove, like honeysuckle on a fence row.

"Phew!" said Lisa. "What's that awful smell?"

"Cows!" Enoch said excitedly, and he put his head out the window and inhaled deeply. It smelled like fresh baked bread to him, like split green wood, like hay bales in a loft.

"A whole truck full of them," said Craig. "Roll up your window."

Enoch closed his eyes and breathed in the sweet air . . . fresh milk, warm and foamy . . . new cut hay . . . pork sausage on a frosty morning.

"For god's sake," said Lisa, her hand over her nose. "Roll up that window."

"Follow it, Craig," said Enoch, pulling his head in. "It's turning right."

"What? The truck?"

"Yeah, it's turning right."

"Are you crazy?"

"Please," said Enoch and leaned out the window again.

"We got to get to school, man. We can't go chasing a truck full of cows. What for, anyway?"

"It smelled so good," said Enoch, pulling his head back in and rolling up the window. In his chest there was a little pain, a catch, like crying.

"I don't believe it," Lisa said, putting a hand to her forehead and leaning back dramatically against the headrest of her seat. "I just don't believe the things you say."

NINE

Enoch could not understand why the teacher would leave the room even for a minute. As soon as he stepped out the stirring started. Cheat sheets were pulled from shoes, shirt sleeves, pants pockets, shirt pockets, purses. Information passed in whispers from desk to desk. The answer to number three was "anaerobic." Number seven was "xylem," not "phloem." People handed their papers to their neighbors or held them over their shoulders for those in back to copy. Enoch tried to ignore it all. There were others like him. A few. Holly Montgomery across the aisle was honest. He had noticed that about her on the last test. That was one of the things he had noticed about her. The first thing he had ever noticed was that she looked good. Not a Rita, but good. Rita, after all, was exceptional. There were other things about her, things that reminded him of people at home, things he could not define precisely, things perhaps in her manner, or in the way she dressed. And she was smart. He had noticed that. She did not need to cheat. So why all of sudden was she talking to Wilson? Was she giving him answers? Why give anything to that smoothie?

Good. She was covering her paper.

"Do your own work," she said softly.

"Come on, Holly," said Wilson. His desk was across the aisle from her on the other side. "Don't be a nurd. Let me see it. Just for a second."

"No," she said. "I mean no."

"Goddamn bitch," he said, lunging out to grab the paper from her desk. She whipped it away and held it beyond his reach. Marianne, in the desk in front of Holly, turned swiftly and pulled it from her hand.

"Here you go, Wilson," she said, holding it up away from Holly. But then Enoch's hand came tight around Marianne's wrist.

"Give it back," he said. Marianne froze, looking stupid and startled.

"Thanks," said Holly, taking back the paper from the captured hand. Enoch let go and sat back down in his seat.

"You hurt my arm, you turkey," snarled Marianne. She would have said more except for a low breathy whistle that came from a desk near the door. Immediately the class became still, the students bending over their work, chewing their pencils in quiet concentration. Mr. Poole, returning to the room, could see the wisdom of his classroom philosophy: Trust them and they will be trustworthy.

When the bell rang, Enoch was still drawing his cross-section of a plant stem. He hurriedly sketched in the rest of it, scribbled in the names of the parts, and located them with quick, sloppy arrows. He was one of the last ones to turn in his paper.

Holly was waiting in the hall.

"How did you do?" she asked. She had never spoken to him before today.

"All right," he said. "I think I did all right." He was pleased that she had waited for him.

"Thanks for helping me out," she said.

"They shouldn't cheat off you if you don't want them to," he said.

"They don't care. All they want are the answers."

"I can't get used to it," he said. "Back where I come from we never even thought about cheating."

"Where was that? Another planet?"

"It seems like it sometimes. Where's your next class?"

"Ms. Chapin. Two-oh-two."

"I go a little way in that direction," he said, and they began walking together down the hall. He liked it, walking with a girl. He tried not to go too quickly.

"Really," she said. "Where is it that nobody cheats?"

"Swallowfield," he said. "Nobody's ever heard of the place, so don't feel bad. It's up in the mountains. I went to a little private school, a one-room deal. Well, two rooms, really. Two teachers. But only about fifteen students."

"A high school?"

"All ages," he said. "Three to fifteen."

"Three?"

"That's Dee and Dum. They're almost four now. They're the teachers' kids."

"Dee and Dum? Those are names? Are they twins?"

"Yeah, Tweedledee and Tweedledum." Enoch laughed because Holly was laughing. "Their names are really Roland and Robert, but nobody calls them that. Their mama tries to, but nobody pays attention to her, not even the twins. We have lots of funny nicknames back home. Like Gladys instead of Galadriel."

"Galadriel the elf queen?" said Holly. "Tolkien?"

"That's right," said Enoch. It pleased him that she knew it.

"Somebody named their kid after an elf?"

"Well, not just any elf. Galadriel had a lot of class."

"I know," said Holly, laughing. "But they changed it to Gladys?"

"Yeah, other people did. Not the parents. They finally went along with it, though. And with changing Meriadoc to Bubba, too."

"Oh, no," said Holly, still laughing. "A little boy named for a hobbit? Where did you say this place is?"

"Up in the Blue Ridge," said Enoch. "It's just a little place. Kind of backwards, you know." He was slowing up, indicating in the way he moved that he had to turn off now, at the next hall.

"It sounds like a great place," she said, slowing with him and then standing for a moment at the intersection of the hallways.

"I'll tell you about it sometime, if you want."

"Sure," she said. "I do want. Thanks again for helping me with those two bums in biology."

"That was nothing," he said, reluctant to leave but unable to ignore the fact that the halls were emptying. "I'll talk to you later."

"Later," she said, and then they were both hurrying away and the bell was ringing for the next class.

For the rest of the day Enoch hoped to catch sight of her

133

between classes. She was nice looking. He wanted to look at her again. She was easy to talk to. He liked the way she had been so easy to talk to. She knew who Galadriel was. She liked hearing about Kettle Creek. She laughed at it but not as Lisa laughed. Not as Craig and Jay did. She laughed as he did, the way they laughed back home, at themselves.

But he did not see her again until school was out, until he was jammed in the crowded hallway, moving slowly toward the outside door, and he saw her ahead, outside, turning down the walk in front of the school and disappearing from his sight. He started pushing ahead, elbowing, but the crowd packed tighter near the door and he had to wait, moving slowly, so very slowly, while she was walking quickly away, he was sure, though he could not see her.

Then he was out the door and free, and he began running in the direction he had seen her go, looking ahead for her, thinking what he would say: Do you need a ride? Then he saw her and ran faster, bumping people.

"Holly," he said, and he was more breathless than he should have been, his heart beating faster than it needed to. She turned around. "Do you need a ride?" he said.

"Oh, thanks, but no. I've got my bike."

"Oh." And for a moment his disappointment blocked everything. Then he said, "You must not live far."

"About two miles. Not far from you."

"You know where I live?"

"You're Craig Callahan's cousin, aren't you?"

"How'd you know?"

"I don't know. Somebody told me, I guess. Anyway, I live over on Forest."

"Don't you worry about the traffic?" he said.

"On Forest Street?"

134

"No. On your bike. Riding to school."

"Yeah, it's kind of hairy. I wear a helmet." She held up the yellow bicycle helmet she was carrying. "Not too stylish, I admit. But I've only got one head and I don't want it smashed."

"No," he said. "That would not be good. Definitely no good at all."

A horn was blowing, had been blowing, he hearing it but not listening, not even fully aware of it until Holly looked away to the street.

"Your cousin," she said. "He wants you." Enoch looked and saw Craig's car pulled up at the curb, Craig and Jay inside, Craig blasting away on the horn. Enoch waved to them.

"Better go," he said.

"Better had," she said. "See you tomorrow."

Enoch hurried to the car, and Craig got out to let him climb through to the back.

"Where's Lisa," Enoch said, getting in.

"I don't know," said Craig. "She'll get a ride."

Every day was different. Sometimes Lisa was with them, sometimes not. Sometimes Jay was already in the car, sometimes not. If he was in the car, it meant Craig had left school early and gone to pick him up. Enoch was not sure how he managed it. It seemed to him that Craig must be cutting classes. He had once asked him about it. Craig had shrugged and said sometimes he was let out early from his last period class, if he had finished his work. But one morning Enoch had left a book in the car and had gone out at the ten o'clock break to get it. The car was not in the parking lot. He mentioned it later to Craig. Craig said it was there all along, that he had overlooked it. But the car

135

was not there. Enoch knew it was not. He did not know what was going on, how much school Craig was cutting, but he was grateful that he always came back to pick him up.

"Getting it on with Holly Montgomery, I see," said Craig as they pulled into the traffic.

"Talking to her," said Enoch.

"Nice body," said Jay. "Get her to come to Wonderland some Friday night. We'll give her some hunch punch, get her loosened up for you."

"Sure," said Enoch, flattening the word, making it say nothing. He did not like hearing Holly Montgomery in their talk. He did not like it even though he had been wanting a girl to talk about, some exploits to tell, cleverly, like Jay did, to show them he was manly. But he did not take it up about Holly Montgomery, did not want to talk that way about her. He was glad, though, that they had seen him with her.

Lisa was already home when they got there. They could hear the television going in the den. They had picked up a sack of hamburgers on the way home, and Jay sat down with it at the kitchen table while Craig went to the refrigerator for Cokes.

"Here's a letter, Enoch," Craig said, nodding toward an envelope on the counter by the refrigerator. Enoch went over and picked it up.

"My mother," he said.

"You having a Coke?" said Craig.

"No, I'll get some milk," said Enoch. "In a minute." He went to the table, opened the letter, and sat down to read it. Halfway through the first page he looked up and stared away at nothing.

136

"Anything wrong?" said Jay.

"Luddie Belle died," said Enoch.

"Who?"

"Luddie Belle," he said, and tears welled up in his eyes. He blinked them away.

"Who's that?" said Craig.

"An old woman in Swallowfield. We sold milk to her."

"And you're going to cry about it?" said Jay. "An old woman? Hell, I didn't even cry when my own grandmother died."

"I'm not crying," said Enoch.

"Did she leave you any money?" said Jay.

"Why should she?" said Enoch. "I wasn't kin to her. Besides, she didn't have any."

"At least I made a little off my grandmother," said Jay. "Maybe that's why you're crying."

"That's a hell of a thing to say," said Enoch, and he got up from the table.

"He's just kidding," said Craig, coming over with the Cokes.

"Then why isn't he smiling?" Enoch said, and he turned and left the kitchen.

He went to his room and finished reading the letter. She died at home in her sleep. That was good. The best you could hope for, Lizzie said. The funeral would be on Friday. Today. Probably it was already over. Maybe right now the graveyard crew was shoveling dirt in her grave. Goodby, Luddie Belle.

He got up and went to his window and looked out. It was fall, leaves red and yellow among the green pines. He had hardly noticed the turning. At home he would have been following it every step of the way, from the first sycamore

leaf that changed to the last oak leaf that came fluttering
down on a breeze. Why not here? Why had he not been
watching?

He went to his dresser and rummaged through one
drawer and then another until he found his old red cap, the
one with the frazzled yarn and all the cow hairs and tiny
chips of wood caught in it. He put it on and went downstairs. In the den he stopped and stood looking at the television, at an old Joan Crawford movie. Lisa was stretched out
on the sofa with a bag of potato chips and a Coke. Her eyes
did not move from the set.

"How was school?" he asked.

"Fine," she said.

"How'd you get home?"

"Francie."

"She drives?"

"No, her mama."

"Lisa, can I interrupt you for a minute?"

"What for?" she said, looking at him.

"I just wanted to ask you," he said, "where do you go
around here when you want to be alone to think about
things?"

"I go to my room," she said. "I shut my door and put a
chair in front of it and put a tape in my stereo and listen to
it over and over again."

"What I really want to know is where do you walk," he
said. "Is there any place you can go walking and be kind of
alone?"

"Not around here. There's not any place to walk around
here. I always go to my room." She was watching the set
again.

"Well, I think I'll try walking anyway," he said and went

138

across to the patio door and slid it open and went out.

"See you later," she said as he closed the door behind him.

He walked around to the front. There was no sidewalk, so he walked along the street. The air was cool with sun-warmth in it. The sky was blue, the deep blue that comes only in autumn. At home in the woods the leaves on the ground would be ankle deep, crisp against his shoes. Here they were raked up week by week and tied in plastic bags and left at the curb in big shapeless bundles. Everything was that way, well managed but lifeless. He looked at the houses as he passed them. They all looked different, and yet there was a sameness to them. All of them were big, no cozy little cottages. They all had dens and studies in addition to living rooms, dining rooms in addition to kitchens, at least two bathrooms, wall-to-wall carpeting, sliding glass doors, patios, decks, and carports. And neat, well-kept yards. No evidence of activity, no vital signs. No ax in a chopping block, no clothes on a line, no path to the house next door. It was all dead, as dead as Luddie Belle. Deader.

Forest Street. The sign on the corner announced it. He had been wondering where it was, if he would come to it. Maybe he would walk down it. But which way? No matter. He would not know her house if he saw it. Except there were mailboxes along the street, names on some of them. But he would never go ring the bell and ask for her. Yet he could at least see what her house looked like. If he found it. If he turned the right way. If the name was on the box.

He turned left because it looked like there were more trees hanging out over the street that way, more leaves to kick through. Forest Street was older than the street Craig lived on. The houses were smaller, the trees bigger. He

139

tried to be nonchalant about the mailboxes. Only a small chance he would find her house. Probably it was back the other way.

But there it was: Montgomery. Right there. Third house. He could have read the box from the corner if he had tried. That was it, where she lived. Just a house. Nothing dazzling about it. A bit shabby even, though not by standards back home. On Kettle Creek it would be princely. But here it looked in need of fresh paint. And the yard was scruffy, as if except for an occasional summertime pass of the lawn mower it was left to take care of itself, to grow into what it wanted to. The leaves were nice and deep.

He kept moving, not stopping to stare. He had a feeling someone was in the backyard. There was a dog back there barking and carrying on: happy barking like Soupy did when someone went out and paid attention to her. So he kept moving. But when he got past the house, he turned and looked into the backyard, what he could see of it, and Holly was there, playing with the dog.

Enoch did not even hesitate. He turned from the street and headed straight for her, across the side yard and into the back, as if she were someone he had known a long time, someone like Gyp or Gladys. It was seeing her again that made him bold. She seemed like someone from home.

When she saw him coming, she waved, then self-consciously picked up a stick the dog had dropped at her feet and threw it again, the dog bounding after it. Then she turned back to Enoch. When he came within hearing range, she said, "I told you I didn't live far from you."

"It wouldn't be far back home. But I'm not sure my cousins have ever walked this far. Nobody walks anywhere around here. There aren't even any sidewalks."

140

"The automobile reigns," she said.

Then Enoch noticed the woodpile. Not a small one like his aunt and uncle had in their carport for the occasional fire in the fireplace. This was a serious woodpile. At least three cords.

"What do you use the wood for?" he said, going over to it and feeling it, smelling the aroma of it.

"Our wood stove," she said. "We heat with it."

"Really? With a wood stove? All your heat?"

"It works good," she said. "Keeps us plenty warm. Wood heat is nice. I know it sounds dumb, but it's different from the old electric heat we used to have. Better. I don't know how to explain it."

"I know what you're talking about," Enoch said. "We use wood back home." He sat down on the woodpile and picked up a piece of hickory. He smelled the split side of it. Then he held it down and looked at it, turning it in his hands. "A friend of mine just died," he said.

"I'm sorry," said Holly, and she sat down, too. She said nothing more, asked no questions. But he felt she cared.

"Her name was Luddie Belle," he said. "She was eighty-six years old and lived in a little tiny house up on a steep hill behind Swallowfield. She was a nice old lady. Real lively and sharp. She talked to kids like they were grown-ups. You always felt easy around her. She'd tell you what she thought, too, straight out. No pussyfooting. She didn't want me to come to Raleigh. She didn't like it at all. She told me so about a half a dozen times. But I came anyway, and now she's dead. I wish it hadn't worked out that way. I wish I could have gone home and talked to her one more time."

Holly did not say anything. But it felt all right, the si-

141

lence did. He ran his hand slowly back and forth over the bark of the wood.

Then she said, "What's it like back there? Somebody told me you're from a commune."

He shrugged. "It's not a commune. We don't own anything together or live together or anything like that. We're just a community. We get together a lot. And we have our own school. But anybody can come to it if they pay their tuition. Like Bethie and Steve Iverson. Their folks are just regular straight people. Old-time Swallowfield. But the Iversons wanted their kids in a school close to home, and they knew Bill and Melinda, and they liked them."

"Who are Bill and Melinda?"

"The teachers."

"Dee and Dum's parents."

"That's right," said Enoch.

"Are they real teachers? I mean, certified and everything?"

"Yeah, they used to teach in public schools."

"And now they just teach that little bitty school? And make a living at it?"

"Almost. Bill does carpentry work in the summers. And they farm some. They get by. Nobody makes very much money back there. Not like around here."

"What do your folks do?" she asked.

"We grow sorghum—"

"Like for syrup?"

"Yeah. It's sorghum time right now, in fact. It brings in our biggest chunk of money. It's not all that big, though. Then we keep a few dairy cows. Just a few. Three or four. We sell the milk to regular customers and that keeps a little pocket money rolling in. And then my mother substitute teaches some. A lot in the winter, when all the teachers get the flu. And my daddy works some at a sawmill. And he does a little carpentry. We get by all right."

Holly's dog came to her with a stick in his mouth, and she took it from him and threw it.

"My mama's a teacher, too," she said as the dog ran out across the lawn. "A regular one. High school history."

"At our school?" said Enoch.

She shook her head. "Across town."

"How about your father?"

"They're divorced. But he works for a big company that makes parts for things. Computer parts, things like that. It doesn't sound too thrilling to me, but he seems to like it."

"There'd be worse things, I guess," said Enoch.

"Growing sorghum in the mountains sounds better. Why'd you leave?"

"I don't know," he said. "To see what it's like out here, I guess."

The dog brought the stick back, and Holly took it from him and put it behind her. Then she coaxed him into lying down at her feet.

"And how is it out here?" she said.

"Parts of it are all right," said Enoch. "But there's something missing. I don't know. It's starting to seem kind of boring. Like, I keep asking my uncle if there's any work he needs done. So finally he lets me rake leaves last Saturday, but it's not that he needs for me to. Usually he hires somebody, he says. It's like he's doing me a favor."

"Craig doesn't rake leaves?"

"He says his old man's got the dough. Let him hire a lackey."

"So he hired you."

"Well, I did it for free. They're feeding me, after all, sharing their house with me. Anyhow, I was glad for something to do. I'm getting a little tired of watching television and riding around in Craig's car. That's all we do besides eating and sleeping and going to school."

"What did you do back home?"

"Worked. Went hunting. Visited people. Read."

"Watched television?"

"Nope. No TV."

"None?"

"We have one TV on Kettle Creek. Bill and Melinda keep it in a closet and bring it out for great events, like presidential inaugurations and impeachments."

"That's all?"

"Just about. Sometimes we go to Gyp and Liddle's grandparents' house and watch other things. But not much. Mostly we read. In my house we read out loud to each other. Especially Mercy, my little sister. She loves it. She'll read to the cat and dog if nobody else wants to listen. She has great delivery. In school even the little kids pay attention when she starts reading."

"Yeah, but no TV. What about news? Don't you need to keep up with things?"

"We do keep up. We read newspapers. We have radios."

"I don't think I would like it, not having TV."

"I know," said Enoch. "Everybody thinks that. I was really looking forward to TV when I came here, but now I don't know. The regular programs are so dumb. I just can't get used to them. And the commercials. There's so much propaganda in them. I start feeling sometimes like I'm in Russia. The oil companies, for instance. What are they advertising for? They aren't trying to sell oil. Watch their commercials sometime. What they're trying to do is sell their whole way of doing business. They tell us how great it is to have big conglomerates running everything. Like they're afraid if they don't tell us how wonderful it all is, we might think for ourselves and decide it's not."

"You ought to talk to my mama," said Holly. "Y'all would get along great. The two things she really gets mad about are giant conglomerates and television."

"I guess a lot of people do."

"But nobody does anything about it," said Holly.

Enoch took off his cap and ran his fingers through his hair. Then he turned the cap in his hands, looking at it, studying the little pieces of Kettle Creek embedded in the yarn.

"You know," he said, "I don't know if I can make you believe this or not, but Kettle Creek is real different from around here. It's sort of like we did something about those things. And it's better. It's better like you were telling me wood heat is better."

"But what did you do?" said Holly. "The conglomerates are still around, running everything."

"But not so much on Kettle Creek. We don't have television telling us what to do and how to think. And we don't have all that stuff the big corporations want us to buy, stuff like my cousins have, like that huge house they live in and all those stereos. You can't feel anything in that house. It's like there's a divider between you and the world. You have to look out the window to see that fall has come. Do you understand what I mean? You have to look out the damn window."

Holly reached out with her foot and rubbed the dog's head.

"It's as if you've come out of the old days," she said. "It amazes me."

"Not the old days," he said. "If you could go to Swallowfield, you'd see. The Nashes live in an octagonal house. They built it themselves. It's got a big solar collector on top that works really well, better than ours does, anyway. At our house we've got a kind of half-assed one for heating our water."

"Don't you have electricity?"

"Some of us do, some don't. My daddy likes not having it, but he's not a fanatic about it. He says we'll put it in if we ever need it. Mountain Man doesn't have it either. And Rita doesn't. But everybody else does. Even the Nashes. That solar collector doesn't do everything. They don't use much electricity, though."

"So you don't have a refrigerator in your house? You don't have lights?"

"We have a springhouse to keep things cold. And we use kerosene lamps. But I'm not against electricity, personally. I think if everybody used it just for small jobs there'd be enough to go around. It's making heat with it that costs so much. And running air conditioners."

"We don't have air conditioning," said Holly, "and we heat with wood."

"Then you're better off than my cousins," said Enoch. "And you ride a bicycle, too."

"And on my bike I see the seasons change," she said.

Enoch turned his hat once more in his hands and then put it back on his head.

146

"Would you be interested in doing something tonight?" he said. "Maybe go to the football game?"

Holly looked at him and smiled. "Yes, I would."

"I don't have a car. We'll have to walk."

"That's okay," she said. "Two miles isn't all that far."

TEN

Outside it was cold and raining. Enoch stood by the wood stove, turning first his front and then his back to it, soaking up the heat. Holly had gone to the front window again and was looking down the street.

"This is going to be a different Thanksgiving," she said. "I promise you."

"You keep saying that," said Enoch.

"I just want you to be prepared. We probably won't even have turkey. Daddy's not much for tradition."

"We don't need turkey," said Enoch.

"Have you ever had Thanksgiving without it?" said Holly.

"No."

"See there," she said, pacing nervously toward the stove, then turning back to the window again. "He's going to be too strange for you. He'll feed you steak and talk computers with you."

"I'm looking forward to meeting him," Enoch said, not entirely truthfully. "I think we'll have a fine day."

"You think so?" She looked quickly at him and smiled. "Maybe we will." Then she looked out the window again. "What's usual for you at home? To have a big gathering?"

"Pretty big," said Enoch. "Most of the people that don't go away to their relatives get together at one house or another. I think the Stroupes are having it this year."

"Well, this isn't going to be anything like that. I'm afraid you'll get homesick."

"No, I won't," said Enoch. But already he was. This was not starting out like Thanksgiving at all.

Holly looked at her watch. "It's time," she said, and she turned anxiously back to the window. "I wonder where he is. You don't suppose he forgot?"

Enoch laughed and went over to stand by her, putting his arm around her. She reached an arm around his waist and squeezed him.

"I always get excited when I'm waiting for him," she said. "I'll calm down after he gets here." She held onto Enoch, looking out.

"Oh, there he is," she said and pulled away from him. In nervous haste she smoothed her clothes and fluffed up her hair. "Do I look okay? Is my hair all right? It's not drooping too much, is it, on this side over here?"

"It looks fine," said Enoch, wondering at her.

She hurried to the front door and opened it and waved at the car that was pulling up in the driveway. Then she turned back to the room, shutting the door against the cold, her hand still on the knob.

"Mama, we're on our way," she called.

"Okay, Holly, just a second," came Nina's voice from the back of the house.

"Don't forget your coat," said Enoch, picking it up from the sofa.

"I already had," she said, and she took it from him and put it on, pulling her hair carefully from beneath it. "Do I still look okay?"

"You look great," said Enoch. He was getting tired of telling her so.

"You two have fun," Nina said, coming into the living room. She was herself, not changed and strained like Holly. Enoch was glad of her presence and was sorry to be leaving. "I'll look for you—what, about seven?" she said.

"I guess so," said Holly. "If it's going to be later we'll call."

"Well, tell Ray I said hello."

"I will," said Holly. "And you tell all the folks at Grandma's that I'll see them at Christmas." She opened the front door, hesitated, and then looked around at Enoch. "Are you ready?" she said.

"Is this supposed to hurt or something?" he said.

"No, silly. Come on."

Her nervousness was contagious. Enoch did not feel easy as he hurried after her through the lightly falling rain to the new Buick, dark red, the rain rolling in beads over its shiny waxed surface. Ray Montgomery reached across the front seat as they approached and opened the door on the passenger side. Holly slid in first, unusually vivacious as she greeted and kissed her father. Enoch got in after her, shivering in the damp coldness. The car at least was warm.

"Daddy, this is Enoch," Holly said brightly.

"Good to meet you, Enoch," said Ray, extending his hand.

"Enoch Callahan," Holly added as they shook hands in front of her.

150

"Nice to meet you, too," said Enoch, feeling a stifling dullness settling in. Ray looked like his car, smooth and correct. Enoch could think of nothing more to say. He sat back, thinking how different Holly's mother was, wondering how those two could have ever been married.

"Enoch's from the mountains," Holly said to her father. "But he's been living here with his aunt and uncle since school started."

"Yes, I believe you were telling me that on the phone," said Ray, backing the car from the driveway. "You're not too homesick, are you, Enoch?"

"No, sir," said Enoch. "Not at all." But saying it made him gaze ahead at the rain being swept from the windshield and think about the Stroupes' house above their store in Swallowfield, about all the people who were gathering there at this very moment.

"Enoch, have you ever seen one of these?" said Holly.

He looked at the dashboard, at the panel of buttons she was pointing to. She pressed the "On" button, and two sets of electronic numbers appeared on little screens.

"What's it for?" he said.

"You've never seen an on-board computer?" said Ray.

"This is my first," Enoch said good-naturedly.

But Ray was completely serious. "It's especially good for long trips," he said. "You feed the data into it, you see, with the numbered keys here. So say you're going to Washington, D.C., and you know it's two hundred and fifty miles. You punch that in like this, see. Two-five-oh. Here's your distance key. And then the time. But here, let's do it for real. Let's clear it and put in the miles we have to go to my place. That'll be eight miles. And get the time right. Now, all you've got to do, Enoch, when you want to know how much farther it is, is punch one of these keys here, this one for distance to go, and this one for ETA. That's Estimated Time of Arrival."

"Like this?" said Enoch and he pushed the distance-to-go button. 7.5 appeared on the screen above, then ticked down to 7.4 . "Pretty good," he said. "What else does it do?"

"It tells you your gas mileage," said Holly. "And how much it's costing you per mile."

"How does it know?"

"You have to give it the facts," said Ray.

"So it only does the math for you."

"That's all, basically," said Ray.

"I thought maybe it was like on an airplane or a spaceship or something, that it would tell you about malfunctions, like that the carburetor mixture was too rich and was fouling the plugs."

"They haven't come up with anything like that yet," said Ray. "Maybe in the future."

"Of course, you can check the spark plugs yourself and see if they're fouled," said Enoch. "You don't really need a computer to tell you."

There was a silence, long enough for Enoch to wonder if he had said something wrong.

Then Ray said, "You seem to know about cars."

"I guess I know a fair amount," said Enoch. "Back home I always helped my daddy work on the truck and the tractor. That's how I learned. Most stuff that came up we could handle. Now and then, though, we'd have to call in Mountain Man."

"Mountain Man?" said Ray.

"That's his nickname."

"He sounds like a real character," Ray said and in his tone was condescension, unintended, but it was there.

"He knows an awful lot," Enoch said, but he knew he could not make it clear that Mountain Man was more than just an interesting character. He turned away and looked out the window at the city in the rain.

"Mountain Man was a lot of help to Enoch's people when they first moved up there," said Holly, sensing Enoch's feelings and trying to set things right.

"Is that so?" Ray said, but there was no interest in his voice, and Holly, too, fell silent.

Enoch glanced at the on-board computer, at the miles ticking off: 5.2 . The digital clock on the dashboard said 11:40 . This would not be over for seven more hours.

"That computer you were talking about, Enoch," said Ray, going back to a topic he cared about. "That might have to wait for new automobile technology. In an electric car, for instance, it would be easy to monitor functions, especially if the car were designed with that in mind. I wouldn't be surprised to see it. The electric car, you know, has quite a future. It's going to be our number-one means of in-city travel one of these days."

"I think it'll be public transportation," said Holly. "Buses and things."

"No, I can't see people giving up the freedom of private cars," said Ray. "There aren't even any plans for that. People wouldn't stand for it."

"I don't know," said Holly. "I like to think of us someday having a bus system that covers everybody, that takes in every single street. Maybe they'd only have little buses for feeder routes, and those wouldn't run as often as the big buses on the main routes. Those little ones could even be some kind of horse-drawn vehicles."

"To save gas, you mean?" said Ray.

"That's what I'm thinking."

"But what about the hay those horses would eat? It takes energy to grow that. Do you have any idea how much petroleum it takes to make fertilizer?"

"You could collect the manure," said Enoch. "Let the horses fertilize their own hay."

"But they're not standing in a barn," said Ray. "You'd have to pay somebody to sweep it up from the streets. And then you'd have to transport it back to the fields. And spread it. And then sow the hay and cut it and bale it and transport it back to town. So where are your energy savings?"

"Yeah, I guess I see your point," said Holly, abandoning the argument.

Enoch thought she could have said more for herself, like that the energy in her plan was human and animal energy and would not have to be purchased from other countries. She would say things like that if she were herself. But obviously she was anxious to please her father. She was not herself and he felt apart from her. He glanced at the on-board computer: 2.3 miles to go. The digital clock said 12:03 . He had liked her idea of the horses. It would be nice to have them clop-clopping along the side streets of Raleigh.

For a little while they did not speak, but rode in silence, not comfortably but in the strained silence of people not used to each other. Then, with .8 miles still to go, they turned off the main road and entered Century World. A large chrome-colored sign named the place, and beside the sign was a sculpture that looked like a hydrogen atom. Just beyond the entrance the road forked, and there were tiers of little signs hanging down to point the way to the pool, the tennis courts, the model units, the sales office, the bath house, the resident manager, the bike paths. Ray took the right fork, toward the tennis courts and sales office. As they drove slowly along, Enoch could see clusters of modern-looking two-story buildings through the rain and the trees. They went three-tenths of a mile and then pulled into a small parking lot. The on-board computer said they were not there yet, still .5 miles to go; but it was wrong.

"There's an umbrella in the back seat," Ray said as he switched off the engine. "Why don't you two use it? No sense in all of us getting wet."

"I don't mind a little water," said Enoch. "You and Holly take it."

"I don't want it," said Holly. "If we can't all be dry, we'll all be wet. Let's make a run for it."

"Where to?" said Enoch, opening his door. The rain was not falling very hard.

"There," said Holly, pointing to the cluster of buildings nearest them. She scrambled out after Enoch and ran a little in front of him, leading the way into the carefully landscaped courtyard, dashing up the steps of its different levels and coming finally to a breathless halt under a little overhang in front of her father's door. Enoch was right behind her, and they turned together and looked for Ray and saw him coming along more slowly. He had the umbrella.

Enoch shivered, thrusting his hands deep in his pockets. He looked around the place. Five units shared the court-yard, making this a little neighborhood. A barbecue pit was in the center with two picnic tables near it. That little cooking-out area looked forlorn in the cold rain, but it was the only sign that people lived here. All the rest was an immaculate arrangement of terraces and shrubbery and at-

tractive rock borders. There were no children's toys or forgotten tools left out, no wheelbarrows or ladders or garden
hoses.

Enoch stepped aside to let Ray come through with the
keys and then watched him unlock three locks.

"Do you have many burglaries around here?" he asked.

"We get hit occasionally," said Ray. "They broke into
number three last summer.

Enoch looked at the front door. Ray was number five.
"What'd they take?" he asked.

"I never heard," said Ray. "The police came around asking questions, but I couldn't help them. I wasn't here when
it happened."

"Who lives in number three?" said Holly. "Are those the
people that put pink bows on their poodle?"

"No, they're next door here, in number four. I don't think
they have that dog anymore. I don't hear it barking like I
used to. I don't know who lives in number three. Some
woman. I never see her." He opened the door and stepped
back, and Enoch followed Holly inside.

It was warm compared to outside, but not as warm as in
the car. Enoch was reluctant to take off his jacket. His head
and feet were wet and cold. He stood in the foyer and
looked around for a fireplace, or maybe even a wood stove,
some source of warmth to stand next to. But there was
nothing like that. He thought of not surrendering his jacket
to Ray, who had just taken Holly's coat and was turning to
him to take his. But that would be impolite, and so he
slipped it off and handed it over. He followed Holly into
the living room and then wandered toward the kitchen as if
looking around the place, but actually checking to see if the,
oven might be on. But he could not find an oven. It took

156

him a moment even to recognize the range, one of those ceramic things that looked more like a countertop than a stove. The oven was not below it. Instead, above the stove where the exhaust hood should have been was a microwave oven. That was no help for warming up. It had a digital clock: 12:34 .

Holly was talking to him now, asking him if he had ever seen such a fancy intercom, and he looked over and saw her fooling around with an elaborate box of dials and controls on the wall. She was explaining about the radio in it with the special weather band and storm watch alarm, but Enoch only half listened as he began looking around the baseboards for a heat vent.

"And see here, it has a little cassette recorder in it for leaving messages," Holly said.

Enoch looked again at the intercom, thinking vaguely that Ray had no one to leave messages for. Then he remembered there had been a second wife, the one Ray married after Nina, and he thought maybe those two had recorded messages to each other, maybe more and more hateful ones until finally she moved out. There was a digital clock on the intercom: 12:38 . He had located the heat vent, and now he moved to stand over it, but only tepid air was wafting up, not enough to warm him through and through.

Holly smiled at him. "Cold?" she said. "I always am when I'm here. But he won't turn up the thermostat. He gets these monstrous electric bills."

The television clicked on in the living room.

"Football," said Ray, coming into the kitchen. "What would Thanksgiving be without it? Can I fix you kids something to drink? Coke? Ginger ale? I've got beer and wine. You can have some of that if you want."

"I'll take ginger ale," said Holly, smiling her too bright smile. She went to her father and put an arm around him, hugging him.

He returned the hug, obviously feeling a wave of tenderness. "So how's it going, doodlebug?" he said. "How's school this year? What courses are you taking?"

And then Enoch realized that Holly had not seen Ray since before school started. He was embarrassed for her. She had not told him, had not wanted him to know how seldom she saw her father, who lived only eight miles away. And now Ray was letting it out. Enoch excused himself, asking the way to the bathroom.

"Down the hall and on your left," said Ray. "What can I get you to drink while you're gone? Some beer? It goes well with football."

"Ginger ale sounds good," said Enoch, leaving the kitchen and going into the living room. On television a woman sports announcer was interviewing a football player in a pregame show. Just below the volume control was a digital clock: 12:45 . Six hours to go.

"I think I *will* have a beer, Mr. Montgomery," Enoch called back into the kitchen.

"Thataboy," answered Ray.

Enoch went down the hall and into the bathroom. Turning on the light, he discovered an infrared heat lamp beaming down from the ceiling. For a long time he stood beneath it, soaking up the warmth. But still, deep down, the coldness remained.

For dinner they had shish-kebobs charcoal-broiled on a countertop grill that had an exhaust fan beside it to draw off the smoke and the fumes. While they ate, they watched football, and after dinner they lounged in the living room

158

and watched more football. When they spoke, they spoke of football. The lively brightness that had earlier been in Holly went slowly out of her, and Enoch watched the digital clock on the television set and waited for it all to be over.

At five thirty Ray sat forward in his chair, put his hands on his knees, and looked at them with interest.

"What say we take off now?" he said. "If we get going before dark, we can go around the long way and show Enoch where I work."

"That sounds good to me," said Enoch, pleased to be going home. Then he glanced at Holly, afraid he had spoken too eagerly. But she met his glance with warmth, and he felt close to her again. She, too, seemed glad to be going home.

The rain had stopped and the clouds were breaking before the sunset, letting through shafts of yellow light. In the soft comfort of the dark red Buick, Holly leaned against Enoch and held his hand, winding her fingers in and out of his. She seemed sad to him, but he understood her better now than he had earlier when she had been too bright and lively and he had not known why.

"There it is," Ray said, pointing to a cube-shaped building up ahead. "That's it. In that building we make some of the most sophisticated electronic components in the whole country. In the whole world, for that matter."

"It looks interesting," said Enoch, and Holly squeezed his hand in sympathy.

"They make computer parts for the space program," she said.

"For other industries as well," said Ray. "But it's space

that interests me. Holly knows that, don't you, doodlebug? That's where the thrill is. Take the space shuttle, now. It's the beginning of a whole new technology. We'll soon be having factories in space, making things up there we could never make down here. It's gravity, you see, Enoch. Up there, with gravity out of the way, we can make alloys from metals that just won't mix down here. We can make new kinds of glass, all sorts of materials we've never seen on earth. Just think of it. It will be like going from the stone age to the iron age in our lifetimes."

"You skipped the bronze age," said Holly.

"Never mind. Just think of the new technology. Enoch, that's why I tell Holly to go into engineering. Get in on some of this. These new materials are going to change our lives, revolutionize everything—from washing machines to guided missiles."

"Now, do you believe that, Enoch?" said Holly. "Do you believe they're going to be making washing machines in space?"

"That's not exactly what I was saying," said Ray.

"I don't know whether I believe it or not," said Enoch. "But I'll tell you what it makes me think of. It makes me think of Luddie Belle. Holly knows about her. She's an old lady in Swallowfield who died not long ago. Luddie Belle never had any kind of washing machine until she was forty or fifty years old. I guess it was after World War II when she finally got one. But she told me once—I don't know how we got onto it—but she told me that sometimes she actually missed the old-time way of washing. I didn't believe her, and so she told me to come to her house the next Saturday morning and she'd show me."

"Wait a second," said Ray. "Let me explain what I meant about washing machines."

160

"I want to tell this first," Enoch said determinedly, and Holly squeezed his hand in support. "She told me to come up on Saturday, and so I walked up there, early, about eight o'clock, and I took my little sister with me. I remember we could see the smoke coming up from the backyard before we got there, and we didn't even try knocking at the door— we just went on around to the back. And there she was, sitting on a bench underneath this big old oak tree, and she was leaning over poking up the fire beneath a great big black pot, and there was steam coming up from the water that was heating."

"How'd she fill up the pot?" said Holly. "From a well?"

"No, with the hose," said Enoch. "She used to do it near a spring and dip up the water. But now she's got running water, so she used the hose. Anyway, she told us we were late, and we tried to make up for it by getting busy, bringing her more wood, splitting it up for her and all. Then we sat down with her on the bench and waited for the water to get good and hot, adding a little more wood to the fire as it went along. It took a while and it was nice sitting there, smelling the smoke and feeling the morning air and the sun gradually warming it. I remember there were blue jays fussing and swooping around in that oak tree up above us, and out in the grass a mockingbird was hunting for bugs, raising up its wings the way they do to scare things up and then hopping a few feet and raising them again. I remember that because we talked about why they raise their wings that way."

"Why do they?" said Holly. "I don't get it."

"Well, you know a mockingbird's got a big patch of white under each wing. So if they spread out their wings it would be like a flash of light to the bugs, right?"

"I guess so," said Holly.

161

"And Luddie Belle says that scares them into moving, and the bird sees them move and catches them. I don't know if it's true or not. But anyway, we sat there and watched this mockingbird. And Luddie Belle talked about how Mercy reminded her of her daughters when they were little and how they used to all do the wash outside together, back before they grew up and moved away. We talked on like that until finally the water got hot enough, and we went to work on the clothes. It turned out to be quite a production. By the time we got them soaped and stirred with a wooden paddle-like thing she had and rinsed and wrung out and hung up, it was just about lunchtime. But we had a good time talking and laughing and carrying on. And the outdoors was nice. I could see what she meant about missing it sometimes. I miss things like that myself."

Enoch fell silent as an idea came to him and swept completely over him. Why not go home? Why not go back to Swallowfield? It was more than an idea. It was an illumination. It blocked out Holly and Ray and the car they were in and the streets they were driving through. Whatever had made him think he could not go home?

"You don't mean to be saying it was easier before the washing machine came along?" said Ray.

"It was harder," Enoch said. "Luddie Belle said her hands would be raw after washing for the whole family, especially with that homemade lye soap they used to use."

"Then what's your point?" said Ray.

"Nothing," said Enoch. He was no longer interested. He was thinking about going home, about getting to his house in the evening and seeing lamplight inside and going up the back steps and across the porch and opening the back door and going into the kitchen, and Lizzie and Clark and Mercy looking up in surprise from the table and then jumping up to greet him.

"The point is that easier may not always be better," said Holly. "Isn't that what you mean?"

"I don't know," said Enoch. "Once Luddie Belle got a washing machine, she always used it. So I don't know." He was thinking about sitting down at the table with his family, one of them fixing him a plate of whatever it was they were eating.

"The point I'd like to make," said Ray, "is that I never said that we were going to make washing machines in space. It's only the materials that'll be made up there. And I don't mean a conventional factory, you understand. It's all going to be automated. It'll run by itself. Men will come in now and then from the space shuttle to service it, but that's all. Of course, there will be a place for workers in space. We'll need hundreds of them to go up and build those solar-power satellites." And Ray went on to explain about solar collectors as large as Manhattan Island. But Enoch, with his mind on home, was not listening; nor was Holly, as she leaned against Enoch's shoulder and watched the streets go by in the fading yellow light.

Nina was there when they got home. She had her shoes off and was sitting with her legs stretched out on the couch, reading a book. When they came in, she looked up with amused curiosity.

"A little early," she said. "How was it?" She looked from Enoch to Holly and back to Enoch again.

But Enoch was unsure how Holly handled things between her mother and father. He waited for her to answer, busying himself with taking off his jacket and going over to the wood heater to get warm.

"Painful," said Holly, and in her voice was the pain of which she spoke. It had not been there before. Enoch suddenly was sorry he had not tried harder with her father and made the day easier for her.

"Hey, now," said Nina, sitting around straight, her amusement changing to a kind of cheerful concern. "You're not getting depressed, are you?"

"Don't I always?" said Holly, turning her back on them to hang up her coat in the closet. "As alone as he is in that place, you'd think he would try harder to stay close to his only child. He doesn't even know me anymore. He didn't make the slightest effort to figure out what kind of person Enoch is. He just bulldozes along, assuming everybody's just like he is. It was a disaster."

"It wasn't," said Enoch. "We had a good meal. Watched some good football."

"He doesn't even know I don't like football," said Holly, coming over to stand on the other side of the heater.

"That's not his fault," said Nina. "You ought to tell him."

"That'd be worse," said Holly, and then she smiled a little. "I'd hate to have to talk for six straight hours about computers."

"He loves them gadgets, don't he?" said Enoch, picking up on her rising spirits.

Holly laughed and turned to Nina. "Enoch got culture shock, I think."

"I can well imagine," said Nina, getting to her feet. "Are you two hungry? What about a turkey sandwich and some pumpkin pie?"

"Oh, do you really have turkey?" said Holly.

"Grandma was sure you'd be needing some," said Nina. "She sent me home with a whole grocery bag full of stuff."

"Good for Grandma," said Enoch, and he followed Holly and Nina to the kitchen.

They ate turkey sandwiches with cornbread dressing and cranberry sauce piled on. They ate congealed salad with cherries and celery and pecans in it. They ate huge pieces of pumpkin pie buried under whipped cream. And it all tasted as Thanksgiving supper ought to taste. They sat back afterward with fresh hot coffee and easy conversation, and Enoch felt warm and happy and satisfied. He could not recall now why he had been thinking of going home. It seemed a childish idea, like running home to mama. And after a while, when Nina went to her room and left the two of them sitting alone on the couch, the thought of going home went out of his mind completely.

ELEVEN

For over a month Craig had been coming straight home after school to go through the mail and take out the letters from the principal's office. The letters had been coming at a rate of one a week to alert Craig's parents to the fact that he was approaching the maximum number of allowable absences in his chemistry class. It was strange, then, when a week went by and no letter came.

"I say they sent it to your father's office," said Jay, taking the last piece of pizza from the box. Enoch watched him, feeling that piece should have been his.

"I wish I knew for sure," said Craig. "I'd clear out and not come home until after they've gone to bed tonight."

Sounds of the television were coming from the den—Lisa at her regular after-school activity.

"I'd clear out anyway," said Jay. "Don't take a chance."

"But what can I do on a Friday night without money?"

said Craig. "If I'm here for supper I can get some money from them."

"Unless Ned did get a letter," said Enoch.

"You want money?" said Jay. "Bring along that radio there." He pointed to the radio on top of the refrigerator. "I can get you forty for that."

Enoch looked at him to see if he was serious. He was.

"They'd miss it," said Craig.

"Yeah, but this neighborhood's full of vandals," said Jay. "They're not going to know who took it. It could've been any of a dozen kids."

"Too risky," said Craig. "I'll get Lisa to call him up and feel him out. If he didn't get a letter, I'll eat supper here."

"How's she going to do it without tipping him off?" said Jay.

"She can do it. She's good at things like that."

"Then let's hurry it up," said Jay, pushing back his chair. "We've got errands to run."

Errands. Enoch got up and took his empty glass to the sink. He was excluded from these errands with never an explanation. He had asked Craig about them once, but Craig had been evasive. So Enoch stopped asking questions. He suspected they were selling drugs, and he had no desire to be involved, and yet he resented being cut out. It was the way Jay said "errands," and the way Craig glanced at Enoch, and the way Enoch was then supposed to remove himself from their company as if he had some business of his own; it happened time and again, and it was humiliating.

Enoch put his glass in the dishwasher and followed Craig and Jay to the den, curious himself to know whether Ned had gotten a letter from the school. This might be a good night to eat supper at Holly's.

Lisa was lying in her place on the sofa, drinking a Coke and eating chocolate cookies. There was a soap opera on television, a doctor show. Craig went over to the set and turned off the sound.

"Craig!" Lisa cried. "Turn that up! Right now, Craig!" She got up to do it herself, not taking her eyes from the screen.

Craig stood in her way. "I need you to do me a favor," he said.

"I won't! I won't do it unless you turn that up! It's almost over! Now turn it up, Craig!" She was yelling.

Craig turned it up, but there was no dialogue now, only organ music rising.

"It's over," she said in despair, still watching as the woman on the screen looked at the doctor with tears in her eyes and turned with tragic dignity and walked slowly away. "Now I don't know what he said to her."

"You'll find out Monday," said Craig, and he turned down the sound again. "I need you to call Daddy for me."

"Because there wasn't a letter in the mail?" said Lisa.

"Yeah, they might've sent it to his office. I need to know. You can just call him up and see how he seems. See if he's upset or anything."

"Okay," said Lisa. "But just remember that you owe me a favor." She went to the telephone and sat down in the chair beside it and thought for a minute, her finger crooked against her mouth. Then she began dialing the number.

"I'll ask him what he wants for supper," she said.

She waited a moment while the phone rang on the other end. Then she said brightly, "Betty? This is Lisa. Can I talk to my daddy, please?" There was a long pause, and she looked up at Craig, rolling her eyes. Then her voice went to sweetness. "Daddy? How're you doing?" There was a short pause. "Just fine," she said. "You having a pretty good day? It's Friday, you know. Aren't you glad?" A pause and she laughed. "Yeah," she said, "I know. Listen, I was just wondering what you wanted for supper. I was getting some steak out of the freezer, and I saw some lambchops in there. Do you want lambchops tonight?" Pause. "I do, too. I was hoping you'd say that." Pause. "Well, she told me steak, but I think she forgot about the lamb. We'll surprise her." Pause. "Okay, Daddy. See you in a little bit." Pause. "Yeah, okay. Bye."

She hung up and looked at Craig. "He seemed fine," she said. "He didn't say anything about you. Better run get some lambchops out of the freezer and put that steak back in." She went over to the television and changed channels and turned up the volume. "I've missed the first part of *Gunsmoke*," she complained.

"Thanks, Lisa," Craig said, and he went back to the kitchen with Jay.

Enoch went up to his room. He would have supper at home after all, especially if they were having lambchops.

Either Lisa misread her father or Ned outsmarted them. Enoch was not sure which. But he had barely started into his first lambchop when he saw Ned bring out the letter. Enoch felt as if he himself had been caught. He looked away from Ned and Craig, glanced at Linda, who was glowering at Craig, and then concentrated on his food. Lisa was doing the same.

"Craig, what is it exactly that you do with your time?" Ned said, understating his anger, holding it, seemingly, in reserve. He put the letter on the table.

169

"What do you mean?" Craig said innocently.

"When you're not going to your chemistry class, what is it that you do?"

Craig's innocence gave way to an air of unconcern. "I just mess around," he said.

"That's all? Just mess around?"

"Yeah, that's all, basically."

"So there's nothing pressing that you have to attend to? Nothing like that?"

Craig shook his head.

"So answer a simple question," said Ned, his anger rising. "Just tell me, please, why you have cut that class to the limit? My god, Craig, the year's not half over, and you don't have a single cut left! And where in the hell are those other letters they sent?"

Craig shifted quickly to repentance and hung his head, shrugging defenselessly. "I don't know, Daddy," he murmured. "I'm sorry."

"Stop groveling," Linda said sharply. "It won't do you a bit of good."

Enoch hurried into his second lambchop.

Craig looked up at his father, assessing his position.

"Okay," said Ned. "I'm going to try not to be angry. All right? Let's just talk calmly and reasonably to one another. And we'll begin by you answering my question. Why have you cut that class so many times?"

"I don't know," said Craig. "I guess because it comes at the end of the day. I'm usually sick of school by then and ready to go home."

"But aren't you there after school to bring Lisa and Enoch home?" said Linda.

Enoch kept his eyes down and worked on his baked potato. He did not want to be brought into this in any way.

"Usually I am," said Craig.

"Then you don't come straight home when you cut," said Linda. "Do you hang around the school or what?"

"I go pick up Jay and we drive around, run a few errands."

"What kind of errands?" said Ned.

Enoch began to eat more quickly.

"Not really errands," said Craig. "We stop at different places and visit people. Mostly friends of Jay's. He needs me for getting around, you know. He waits all day for me to come for him. So sometimes I do him a favor and come a little early."

"And meanwhile you're flunking chemistry," said Ned. "And if you flunk chemistry, you won't graduate, and you won't get into college. Don't you think about things like that?"

"I don't know," said Craig. "I'm not so sure I want to go to college next year anyway. I might want to take a year out, like Jay is doing."

"A year out for what?" said Linda.

"To rest. To get my head straight."

"Rest?" Ned said. "You're going to flunk out of high school and then take a rest? And then what? What kind of plans do you have for the future? What do you imagine yourself doing five years from now?"

"What kind of question is that?" said Craig. "How do I know? Nobody even knows what the world's going to be like in five years. We might be back to the Dark Ages. How do you expect me to plan for that?"

171

Enoch finished his last bite and wiped his mouth and put his napkin on the table. "Excuse me," he said quietly, getting up from his chair.

"You can start by not cutting any more classes," Ned said to Craig as Enoch left the dining room. But Enoch knew that Craig would keep cutting, that he would never make it through chemistry, that he was already too far behind.

It was almost midnight when Enoch got home from Holly's that night. He used his key to let himself in the back door. The house was quiet except for the muffled sounds of the television coming through the closed door of Ned and Linda's bedroom beyond the study. The house was warm in contrast to the cold night air he had just walked through, but it was cool enough for him to keep his jacket on as he rummaged through the refrigerator.

The television was suddenly louder, then soft again, the bedroom door opening and closing. Ned came padding in with bare feet, wearing only his shorts, carrying an empty martini glass.

"Well, hello, Enoch," he said. "Didn't hear you come in. Have a good night?"

"Sure did. Got hungry, though, walking in the cold."

"Anything you see there, help yourself," said Ned, pouring himself another drink. "I think there's some of that chicken left over from last night."

"I was thinking about some of this soup," said Enoch, bringing out a jar of bean soup.

"Sure," said Ned. "Go right ahead. Sounds good." He picked up his fresh martini and started back to his bedroom. Then he stopped, and without turning around he said, "You didn't run into Craig tonight, did you?"

"No. Sure didn't. But Holly and I just went to the movies and then to Tony's for pizza. Not much chance we'd run into him, really."

"No, he doesn't do those kinds of things, does he. He does . . . what? Well, who knows, a boy his age. As long as he stays out of trouble. And he does that. So he must be doing all right. Except for that school business. And that's . . . well, who knows, really. We'll see you in the morning."

"Good night," said Enoch, setting the jar on the counter. For a moment he paused, vaguely troubled; then he got out a pan and set about heating the soup.

It was much later, almost morning, when Lisa woke him, shaking him up out of a deep sleep. At first he thought it was morning, but then, not yet fully awake and sensing it was dark, he got confused and thought it was Mercy shaking him, back home in his attic bedroom. Then he opened his eyes and saw Lisa, her face dimly lit by the light that came in from the streetlight outside. She had her finger to her lips, silencing him. He sat up, suddenly awake.

"What is it?" he said, and she clapped her hand over his mouth.

"Be quiet," she whispered, almost soundlessly. "It's Craig. Come on."

"Why be quiet?" he said softly as she moved her hand away.

"Hush!" she whispered. "Don't make *any* sound. None. We don't want Mama and Daddy awake. So just be real quiet and come on."

Enoch pushed back the covers and got up. He was wearing only his long johns.

173

"Better put something on," she whispered. "He's outside."

"Craig is?" he whispered, pulling on his pants and slipping his sockless feet into his shoes. He put on his jacket without bothering with a shirt.

"Better carry your shoes till we get out," she said.

He took his shoes back off and followed her. Ned and Linda's bedroom was separated from theirs by two split levels and the length of the house. There was little chance they would wake them, especially with the carpet soaking up their footsteps. They went out through the den, the glass door to the patio sliding softly open and closed. Lisa waited impatiently while Enoch slipped on his shoes. Then she tugged on his arm to hurry him as he started with her around the house.

"He's in the car," she whispered.

"Is he hurt or what?" said Enoch. "Don't you think we should get your folks?"

"No," she said emphatically.

The car was out by the curb instead of in the driveway. Enoch could see Jay standing beside it.

"Where's Craig?" Enoch asked as they approached. "What's going on?"

Jay said nothing but pointed into the back seat. Enoch looked in and saw Craig lying on his face, one arm hanging down, the other caught under his body, one knee on the floor.

Alarmed, Enoch looked back to Jay.

"We need to push the car into the driveway," Jay said softly. "I didn't want to wake anybody up by driving it in. I coasted here from up the block."

"But what's wrong with him?" said Enoch.

"Drunk. Passed out. What does it look like?"

Enoch looked back in at Craig. "Jesus," he murmured.

Jay went to the back of the car. "Come on, Enoch," he said quietly. "You, Lisa, get in and steer."

So Enoch went around and they rolled the car silently into the driveway to its usual place. Lisa got out and pulled the front seat back. Jay reached in and grabbed Craig's arms and began carelessly pulling him out. Enoch stepped in quickly to take one arm and steer Craig's head clear of the door frame. When they got him out, they turned him over and laid him on his back. With the cold air on his face, Craig opened his eyes, blinking slowly, looking at them blearily, his lips shaping up to speak and then going slack again, his eyes falling closed, flickering open, then closed again. To Enoch he seemed more than drunk.

"Let's sit him up," Jay whispered.

They pulled him up, and Craig's eyes came halfway open. His head lolled forward.

"Think you can walk?" Jay said quietly. Craig nodded.

"He can't," said Enoch.

"If we hold him, I think he can," said Jay. "Let's haul him up."

So they lifted Craig to his feet, supporting him on either side, his arms around their shoulders. They made their way slowly into the house, leaving their shoes outside, half carrying Craig up to his room as Lisa went before them, opening doors. And as they went along so slowly, being so carefully quiet, Enoch grew more and more fearful of the possibility that Craig had overdosed on something besides alcohol.

175

"Let's get your parents," he said to Lisa as they dumped Craig into bed.

"No, Enoch!" Lisa whispered fiercely. "That's the last thing Craig would want. Hasn't he already been in enough trouble today?"

"But what if he's overdosed?"

Lisa looked at Jay.

"He's all right," said Jay. "Just let him sleep."

"Was he taking any downers with the booze?" said Enoch.

Jay shrugged. "How should I know? We were at a party. I wasn't watching his every move."

"Then he could have been?" said Enoch, his voice rising in alarm.

"Hush!" said Lisa, grabbing Enoch's arm and shaking him. "Jay said he'll be all right. He knows."

"He wasn't doing downers," said Jay. "He just needs to sleep." He turned to leave.

Enoch followed him. "Then what? What did he take?"

Jay said nothing, but strode silently through the house to the den and slid open the patio door and slipped on his shoes. Enoch followed him outside, still barefooted, ignoring the cold beneath his feet.

"You know what he took," Enoch said angrily, trailing Jay across the yard. "You know because you gave it to him. You ought to tell us. He could die from it if we don't know." He took a running step to catch up with Jay. "You know what it was, you son of a bitch. I know you do. You're just protecting yourself."

Jay stopped and looked at him, one side of his mouth twisting up into a sneering smile. "He won't die. You can

176

rest your ignorant farmboy mind about that. Now get off it and leave me alone." He turned and walked away down the dark street.

Enoch stood for a moment watching him go, then felt the freezing cold beneath his feet and hurried back to the house.

Upstairs it was dark, no light from beneath the closed door to Craig's room. Lisa had gone back to bed. Enoch opened Craig's door and went in, crossing the room in darkness. He turned on the lamp beside the bed. Craig was lying still, but his eyes were open, fluttering, looking at Enoch. His face was mottled and twisted into an expression Enoch did not know, like Craig's face on another person, a stranger behind it.

"You all right?" Enoch asked, sitting down beside him.

Craig nodded and mumbled something.

"What's that?" said Enoch, leaning closer.

Craig smiled vacantly, his eyes closing. He seemed to be sleeping. For a while Enoch sat and watched his breathing. It seemed short to him, not as deep as it should be. But it kept on, breath following breath. Enoch wondered if there was anything he should be doing, like keeping him awake or making him vomit. But Jay had not said to. The bastard. But he did know about these things and he had not said to keep Craig awake. So let him sleep. Let him sleep it off. Enoch wondered if he should do as Lisa had done and go back to bed. But he watched Craig's chest rise and fall and did not want to leave. Someone should be with him in case the breathing stopped. He still thought he should go wake up Ned and Linda. But Lisa had been so adamant. And probably Jay was right—Craig only needed to sleep. Waking up Ned and Linda might only make more trouble.

Enoch reached over and turned out the light. Through the rest of the night he sat on Craig's bed, awake and thinking, monitoring his cousin's breathing and listening to the silence of the house, to the emptiness of its spaces.

TWELVE

Mercy reached down to the foot of her bed and pulled the comforter over her legs and wiggled closer to the lamplight.

"Okay, cats, pay attention. I'm going to read to you about Lassie the come-home dog."

But Petunia and her kittens kept on leaping and chasing through the attic bedroom, sliding, ambushing, skittering, rolling together in tangled furry balls.

At first Mercy read aloud, but then she fell silent, reading more quickly to herself, anxious to learn if the old couple who had nursed Lassie back to health were going to let her go free. They did, poignantly, and Mercy, lost in the story, wiped a tear from her cheek as she moved with Lassie across the fields, south toward home.

"Let's go, Mercy," Lizzie called up the stairs. "It's quarter to seven."

Mercy looked up from the book, dazed, then remembered the parents' meeting at the school.

"Oh, Mama, do I have to go?" she called. "I'd rather stay home and read."

She heard Lizzie talk to Clark. Then Lizzie said up to her, "All right. If you want to. We'll be back in an hour or two."

"We're locking up," Clark called from the back door.

"Okay, Daddy, thanks. See you." The door closed and Mercy turned back to her book. Petunia was on the bed now, washing, settling down for a nap. The kittens tried to move in to nurse, but Petunia turned away from them, hissing at them when they persisted, for she was tiring of their roughness and greed and was beginning to wean them. They moved away grudgingly and curled up together in a heap.

The house was quiet, a bit lonesome, and Mercy's attention would not return to her book. She thought of the meeting. Everyone would be there, the parents in one of the schoolrooms, the children entertaining themselves in the other. She remembered Effie's talk about a skit, about working it up tonight while the parents met and then performing it for them afterwards.

"I'm going," she said suddenly. Bouncing from the bed, she hurried downstairs and grabbed her jacket from the hook by the door. She ran outside into the cold darkness, down the hill and up the dirt road, hurrying to catch up with Clark and Lizzie.

The call came near midnight. The ringing entered Enoch's sleep and woke him. He heard it keep on, ring after ring, until finally someone answered it. In the quietness that followed he slipped back into sleep. Then his aunt was there, turning on his light, coming over to his bed.

"Enoch," Linda said. "Are you awake?"

"Yes," he said, sitting up. "What is it?"

"Your dad's on the phone," she said, the words thudding into him. "You'd better come talk to him. He's got some bad news."

"Bad news?" he said, and he did not even feel himself rise from the bed, his body gone light with dread.

"Everybody's all right," said Linda. "But your house is gone. Burned."

"Oh, no," Enoch said quietly, putting his hand to his stomach as if he had been hit. Then he was out of the room, running down the hall and down the steps and into the den, grabbing up the telephone receiver.

"Daddy?" he said.

"Here he is," Ned said on the extension in the study. "I'll leave you two to talk."

"Enoch?" said Clark.

"Daddy," said Enoch, breathing hard. "Are you okay? Is everybody okay?"

"We're fine," said Clark and his voice sounded calm and normal. "Nobody was home. Nobody was hurt. No close calls even. It was practically over by the time we got there. Poor Tunia, though. She was inside. And her kittens, too. Course, you didn't know them. I guess Petunia is the saddest part of it right now. The rest hasn't quite sunk in yet."

"It's all gone?" said Enoch, feeling numb, leaden. "Everything?"

"Except what we've got on our backs. And my tool chest, thank God. I'd just put it in the truck after supper, for a job tomorrow. So we've got that and some books out on loan to

181

people, and that's about all. I just wish I had taken my guitar to the meeting like I'd thought about doing. But we've been wishing a lot of things the last few hours. It's not doing us much good."

"So what happened?" said Enoch. He sat down on the edge of a chair, his father's tone calming him somewhat. But still his knuckles were white as he held the receiver against his ear.

"Well, I almost hate to say how it started," said Clark. "Mercy left her lamp on. . . ."

"Oh, god," Enoch said softly. "Poor Mercy."

"Yeah," said Clark. "That's the worst of it. But that's how it started, we're almost certain. She's pretty undone about it."

"Y'all weren't home?" said Enoch. "Where were you?"

"Up at the school. At a parents' meeting. Mercy came late and left her lamp on in her room. And the cats were up there. And I guess they started playing. Those kittens had gotten pretty big. They probably knocked over the lamp. And that was it. Nobody saw it until it was too late."

"Well, are y'all all right? I mean, not too upset or anything?"

"There's been tears," said Clark. "But there's been laughing, too. A giddy kind of laughing. It's been a weird night."

"Sounds like it," said Enoch.

"Mercy's the one taking it the worst. That's what's hurting me right now. If the house is going to burn down, okay. I can live with that. I just wish it could've burned down some other way."

"Is she there?" said Enoch. "Can I talk to her?"

"She's right here," said Clark. "Just a second."

"Your brother wants to talk to you," Enoch heard him

say. There was some shuffling and clunking and then there was Mercy.

"Enoch?" she said in a small voice.

"Yeah, sweetheart. How you doing?"

"Enoch, I burned the house down," she said, starting to cry. "I burned up Petunia and the kittens." Her words came haltingly, choking her. "Everything's burned up. I left the lamp on." She was sobbing now, and Enoch could hear Lizzie's voice in the background. Tears were in his own eyes.

"Mercy, don't cry," he said. "Please don't cry. Listen, I'm going to come home, okay? I'll be home tomorrow."

"Yes do, Enoch," she said so softly he could barely hear her. "Please come home." There was a pause and he could hear her sniffling. Then the receiver clunked and he heard her blowing her nose. Then she was back. "You can't come home. I burned it up," she said ironically, her voice clearer, the crying done. "Burned it to the ground."

Enoch smiled. "A complete job, huh?"

"Everything," she said. "I got it all." There was another pause. "Oh, but the cats," she said, her voice going sad again.

"Hey, Mercy, don't think about it, okay? It was an accident. Don't blame yourself for an accident."

"Yeah, but if I'd done what I was supposed to, it wouldn't have happened. That's the thing, Enoch. That's the whole thing." She was getting teary again.

"Listen, don't be like this, okay? I want you bright-eyed and bushy-tailed when I get there tomorrow. I'll come in on the first bus I can get. I'll be home before you know it."

"And you're going to stay?" she said.

"If you'll quit crying."

"I will, Enoch. I've quit right now. I'm not crying, am I, Mama?"

In the background Enoch could hear his mother say, "Not anymore."

"Let me speak to Lizzie," he said.

"All right," said Mercy. "But hurry home, okay?"

"Sure, sweetheart. I'll see you tomorrow." Then he heard her say, away from the phone, "He's coming home tomorrow," and then Lizzie's voice was in his ear.

"You missed an exciting night," she said.

"You doing okay?" he said.

"I'm feeling surprisingly well. Kind of numb. I mean, it's bad when I think about what we can't replace, the sentimental family things. That hurts. But the rest of it, it's just an inconvenience. It was only stuff. We shouldn't mourn stuff, should we? Poor Petunia, though. We're mourning her. But I guess we're about done with that, even."

"So, where are y'all?" said Enoch. "Where are you staying?"

"We're at the Harrimans' right now, but we'll sleep at Mountain Man's tonight. We'll make less of a crowd at his house. And after tonight, I don't know. We'll work something out. Are you really coming tomorrow?"

"I sure am," said Enoch. "The first bus I can catch."

"That's good," Lizzie said softly. "We want you back. We need you."

"I know."

"Let us know when your bus is getting in. Call here or at the Nashes'."

"Okay, I'll call in the morning."

"We'll be there to meet you," said Lizzie. "Somebody will. And listen, don't lose sleep over us tonight. We're

184

doing all right. We really are. We're all together and we have our friends here."

"I wish I was there, too," he said.

"You're with us in spirit," she said.

"I guess that'll have to do."

"Until tomorrow, anyway. Sleep tight, Enoch."

"Night, Mama. Tell everybody good night."

"Okay, I will. Good night now."

"Night," he said.

He hung up the receiver, and for a few minutes he just sat, trying to fit it all in, to put an empty spot in his mind where the house used to be, pain where Mercy was, crisis where Clark and Lizzie were, death where Petunia was. His mind resisted, wanting it the old way, comfortable and easy. But the old way was gone. Home was not there anymore.

Enoch got up and went to the kitchen. The family was sitting around the table. Craig was eating a piece of cake. They all looked at him when he came in.

"Well, Enoch, it's tough news," said Ned. "Real tough."

"Yeah," said Enoch. "Pretty bad." He leaned against a counter, feeling apart from them.

"They seem to be taking it well," said Linda.

"Except Mercy," he said.

"They didn't get anything out?" said Craig.

Enoch shook his head. "Clark's got his tool chest, is all. It was in the truck."

"He'll need that," said Ned, "if he plans to build back."

"No insurance," said Linda, shaking her head. "I can't believe he didn't have insurance. Just imagine." She looked at Enoch. "I think you can see now why people need insurance. It's a hard way to learn."

185

Enoch said nothing. He looked at her and then at the others. That tone they were using: Clark-the-family-hippie screws up again. And drawing him into it, as if he were with them instead of with Clark. And why not? He was living in their house, proof by his presence that the life Clark had made for him was not adequate. But it was adequate. More adequate than this one. Clark and Lizzie had no insurance because they needed none. They had family strength behind them, and friends, and community. And they were not addicted to stuff. It was not going to take any fortune to build back.

"I'll be going home tomorrow," he said. "First bus I can get. I guess I'd better try to get a little sleep."

"Is there anything we can do for you?" said Linda, feeling his estrangement. "How about some cake and milk? Here, sit down and I'll get you some."

"No thanks. Bed is what I really need. I'll see y'all in the morning."

"Good night, then," said Ned. "If you can't sleep and need somebody to talk to, come get me up. I probably won't be asleep either."

"Thanks," said Enoch and started from the kitchen. Then he stopped and turned back to them. "I want y'all to know that I appreciate everything—y'all sharing your house with me and treating me like one of you. I just want you to know that I'll always appreciate it." Then he turned away from them and went up to bed.

Sleep was far away, unreachable. Enoch lay staring into the darkness, imagining how it must have been—the flames spreading from room to room, destroying place after place that he had known so well. He had to see it all in his mind,

186

each part of it as it burned away. It was like saying good-by. And it was painful, surprisingly painful.

He wiped the tears from his cheeks with both hands. He should not be crying. It was only stuff. Except for Petunia. And she was only a cat. Nobody was dead. They could get more stuff. They could build back. But the old stuff, the old house, it was so comfortable, so familiar. And poor Mercy. Poor, poor Mercy standing there watching it burn, knowing she had done it, that she was to blame. But it was only because she was bouncy and carefree, because she was younger and was used to having Enoch there, watching out for her, reminding her of things. And if he had not been in Raleigh, if he had stayed home where he belonged, the house would still be standing and Mercy would be sleeping peacefully in her bed with Petunia snuggled down in the covers beside her.

Enoch sat up and rubbed his hands hard against his face. Then he got up and went to his window and pulled back the curtain and looked out. The streetlight made everything ugly and harsh, always the same light outside. He never knew the phase of the moon anymore. And what was Holly going to say? What would she say when she learned he was leaving? She was the only good thing he had found in Raleigh.

He took his suitcase from the closet and laid it open on his bed. He was the only one in his family now who owned a change of clothing. He felt guilty for having so much. Maybe he should take just a few things back and have the rest sent later.

But he could share his clothes with Clark. Lizzie could probably wear some of them, too.

187

"Packing up?"

Enoch looked up, startled to find Ned in the doorway.

"Yeah, I couldn't sleep," he said, and turned and took a shirt from the closet.

Ned leaned against the doorway, his hands in the pockets of his bathrobe. "I've been thinking," he said. "You shouldn't have any trouble getting excused from school this week. I'll give them a call tomorrow. With Christmas holidays coming up next week, you'll have three whole weeks at home."

Enoch looked at him. "But I'm not coming back. I thought you understood that. I'm going home to stay."

"Well, I can see why you would say that right now, in the heat of the moment. But I think when you get back there you'll see it differently. There's less there for you now than before. There's not even a house. But here there's your education, so many advantages to consider. And in this house we'll always have a place for you."

Enoch stood looking down at the shirt in his hands. He was aware of his breathing, of his long silence as he searched for concreteness in his thoughts, for a framework from which he could speak.

"I think I have more advantages at home," he said at last. "I think I've had more advantages all along than most of the kids around here."

"Including Craig and Lisa?" Ned said quietly.

Enoch looked at him. His uncle was searching his face, asking for truth. Enoch nodded.

Ned pushed his hands deeper into his pockets and stared down grimly at the floor. "You're probably right," he said.

Enoch opened his mouth to deny it, but then closed it

again. He folded the shirt in half and slowly smoothed out the wrinkles.

"Sometimes I halfway wish I had done what Clark did," said Ned. "I halfway wish I had raised my kids like he raised you. There's a lot to be said for it. I can't deny it. But that would have meant giving up the security of my job, and I don't know that I could have done that. Because what if my house had burned down? What would I have done then? What's Clark going to do, Enoch?"

"Build back."

"With what?"

"I don't know," said Enoch. "We'll figure out something."

For a few minutes they were silent. Enoch finished folding the shirt and put it into his suitcase. Then he took another shirt from the closet and folded it and packed it.

"I guess you hate leaving your girl," Ned said quietly.

"I really do," said Enoch.

"Will you see her before you go?"

"I'm going over there as soon as I can decently call it morning," he said.

Enoch called Holly at five o'clock and woke her up.

"I need to see you," he said. "Can I come over now?"

"Now?" she said. "What's wrong?"

"Wait until I get there. Don't worry, okay?"

"Then hurry, because I am worrying."

"I'll be right there," he said and hung up.

Then he was out of the house, jogging through the quiet streets in morning darkness. She opened the door before he knocked, anxiety in her face. He kissed her lightly.

"I told you not to worry," he said.

"I don't necessarily do what I'm told. What is it? What's wrong?"

He sniffed the air. "I smell coffee," he said.

"I've got some on. Come on to the kitchen."

He followed her across the living room. "My house burned down," he said. "Back home on Kettle Creek."

"Oh, Enoch, no!" She turned to him in alarm. "Your people? Are they all right?"

"Except for the cat. And Mercy, who's all torn up over causing it. I'm going home in a few hours. And I guess I'll be staying there."

"Oh, Enoch," Holly said, sorrow descending on her. She moved blindly to a kitchen chair and sat down. "Oh, Enoch. Look at me, I'm crying. What a mess. Not brave at all. Oh, damn it all, I don't want you to go." And she put her head down on the table and wept. He went and stood beside her, reaching for her, and she turned to him and put her arms around him and cried into his stomach. He held her painfully, not wanting to leave her.

Her sobs slowly subsided and she grew still. Then she sighed and rubbed her face against his shirt, drying her tears. She pulled back and looked up at him.

"I'm crying like a selfish ass," she said. "And here your house has burned down and your family is homeless. Did they get anything out?"

Enoch took her face in his hands and kissed her. Then he stood back from her, one hand still caressing her shoulder.

"Let's have some coffee," he said. "Can I fix us some breakfast? Some eggs or something? Where's your mama?"

"Getting dressed."

"When she gets out here, I'll tell the whole story. But no,

190

they didn't get anything out. Now, what I need is a frying pan and some eggs. And some flour. I make good biscuits, you know."

She smiled at him. "No, I didn't know that."

"You wouldn't happen to have any sausage, would you?"

"Up in the freezer."

"And sorghum syrup?"

She laughed and shook her head. "Honey'll have to do you."

"It'll do," he said, going to the refrigerator and looking up in the freezer for the sausage. "But you ought to keep some sorghum on hand. I'll send you a gallon of it. The best sorghum syrup you'll ever taste. I'll send it to you tomorrow."

THIRTEEN

Enoch awoke, anxious and haggard. He rolled his head slowly to the window and looked out through half-closed eyes at the interstate highway sliding past. In his dream he had been in the burning house. He had dodged flames, jumped over them, turned in terror from blocked doors, and escaped at last through a window, bringing out with him his .22 rifle and the Cherokee basket Lizzie used for gathering vegetables in the garden. Outside he had found his family, all in distress, and Holly had been with them. They had told him to go back in and get the cat.

There was no rest in that sleep. He felt as worn as before. His stomach was sour from too much coffee and from too much grease in the hamburger he had eaten for lunch. Asheville was still an hour away, Fairmont another hour and a half. But the hills were higher now. It was good to be in the mountains again, good for the eye to rise with the land, restful to gaze over the brownness of the pastures and trees. And it would be even better to be off the bus, to be home with his people, to be walking on the earth again, the real earth of fields and woods, to walk the old path again, down by the chickenhouse, past the barn, into the pasture, his feet solid against the frozen ground, to come to Kettle Creek, the trees standing bare above it, the water high and rushing from the winter rains, to feel again its vitality, the living presence of it through the valley, marking the place of which he was a part.

It was four in the afternoon when the bus rolled into the station at Fairmont. Clark's truck was there, parked in front of the station. Enoch felt a thrill at the sight of it. He carefully picked up the knapsack that had been in his lap through the trip and cradled it in the crook of his arm. Then he was up and moving down the almost empty aisle, only a few people deboarding in this little mountain town. As he stepped off the bus, there was Clark, the same as ever in his work pants and plaid shirt and down vest and his cap with the earflaps tied up. Clark was smiling and his hands were out to greet him, ambivalent in their gesture, leaving it to Enoch whether to shake hands or embrace. Enoch embraced him, holding the knapsack out from the crush. Then Clark stepped back and looked him up and down.

"Not much change," he said. "Maybe a little smoother looking."

Enoch smiled and shrugged. "Better get my suitcase," he said. "Hold this," and he held out the knapsack gently in both hands.

"What've you got there?" said Clark.

"You'll never guess," said Enoch, handing it to him.

"Well, I'll be dogged," said Clark when his hands felt it. He pulled back the zipper a little way and looked in. "Just what we needed."

"Don't take her out," said Enoch. "She stays quiet in there in the dark. If you bring her out, she gets panicky."

"Well, I'll be dogged," Clark said again. "Prettiest little kitten I've ever seen." He closed the zipper. "Where'd you get her?"

"Just a second and I'll tell you," said Enoch. "Got to get my suitcase." He stepped over to the baggage compartment of the bus and pointed out his suitcase to the driver.

"She's a gift from a friend of mine," he said as he returned. "Holly Montgomery."

"Is that all you got?" said Clark, nodding at the one suitcase.

"I left a trunk full of stuff there. Ned said they'd send it when we have a place for it."

"You could've brought it," said Clark as they turned and headed toward the truck. "We could've put it in the barn."

"Well, I didn't know," said Enoch.

"Course, it'll make it easier for you to go back if you decide to," said Clark.

"I'm not going back," said Enoch. "I'm definitely not going back."

Clark turned and looked at him. "Definitely not, huh?"

"Definitely," said Enoch, lifting his suitcase into the back of the truck. There was more he could have said, things that were in his mind to say, about this being his home, his place. But all he said, getting into the cab, was, "I'm home to stay."

"Well, I'm glad to hear it," said Clark. He started the engine and backed out into the street.

194

Enoch unzipped the knapsack and took out the kitten and nestled it against his chest, stroking the long red fur.

"Think Mercy'll like her?" he said.

"Are you kidding?" said Clark. "Where'd this Holly person get her on such short notice?"

"She knew some people with a litter of kittens," said Enoch. "She called them up at six thirty this morning, and we went over and picked this one out."

"Six thirty," said Clark. "Sounds like Holly's kind of special."

"Yeah," said Enoch and let the kitten down to walk around on the seat. He did not want to talk about Holly. It made her seem less real to him, less close.

"How's Mercy?" he said.

"Better," said Clark. "She's a tough little kid. And you coming home today has kept her on the cheery side."

"I'm glad," said Enoch.

They were driving out of Fairmont now, into the countryside. As Enoch looked out at the familiar landscape, a contentment settled over him.

"Don't you think it's a good life here?" he said.

"Sure I do," said Clark. "What are you thinking?"

"That if Ned's house burned down and he didn't have insurance, he'd be ruined. But that we've got ourselves to fall back on. We just round up our friends and build something back. Something to keep the rain off. No palace or anything. We didn't need insurance."

"Don't let me hear that from you," Clark said sharply.

Enoch looked at him, startled.

"Don't go romanticizing us not having insurance," said Clark. "Your mama and I were fools not to have insured that house."

195

"Then why didn't you?"

"Some fool-ass romantic notion. Self-sufficient country folks living off the land don't have fire insurance, can't afford it, don't need it—some stupid idea like that. And we figured the house was old, wasn't worth anything. But it was worth something, more money than we can lay our hands on this minute. We've got to come up with it if we want to build back."

"What are we going to do?" said Enoch.

"I start full time at the sawmill next week," said Clark. "I talked to Billy Jenkins today. We're damn lucky. He just had a man quit."

"Full time?" said Enoch. "What about building the house?"

"I'll have to work on it when I can. On weekends at first. When the days get longer in the spring, I can work on it in the evenings. We're in for a hard time of it, I'll tell you straight out. You and Lizzie are going to have to do the farming now. And next fall, if Lizzie gets a full-time teaching job at Fairmont like we need for her to, you'll have to take on most of the farming yourself, you and Mercy, and keep up with your schoolwork, too. It's going to be hard around here. We're going to have to work when we're tired. There'll be short tempers all around. You might get to wishing you were back in Raleigh."

"No, I won't," said Enoch. He picked up the cat and scratched its ears, and for a moment he was thinking of Holly. Yet it felt good to be home, even with all of this.

"I guess we'll insure the new house," he said.

"That's right," said Clark. "We'll close the barn door after the horse is out."

196

For a time they were silent.

Then Enoch said, "Are we going to be living in our barn again?"

"Not until the weather warms up," said Clark. "I think we're going to stay at Rita's this winter."

Enoch looked up abruptly from the cat, feeling a touch of the old rush. "At Rita's? Is there room?"

"She's not going to be there," said Clark. He glanced at Enoch and laughed. "That would be crowded, wouldn't it? She's talking about going down to stay with Bo on a ranch on the Rio Grande."

"Oh," said Enoch. He felt Clark still looking at him, and he met his glance and laughed, flushing a little. "I was wondering."

It was a shock to round the bend on the dirt road and see the house gone from the shoulder of Wolf Ridge. Even Clark murmured at it. All that stood now was the chimney with a great heap of black rubble spread around it. And around the rubble there were pickup trucks, ten or a dozen, backed up, tailgates down. And on top of the rubble were people, lots of people.

"I guess it cooled enough to start clearing," said Clark. "I didn't think we'd be able to start until tomorrow." He turned up the driveway. Enoch was still staring, stunned at the sight of no house.

"It looks so strange," he said. "Like a hole."

"I know," said Clark. "I can't get used to it either."

"Seems silly to start clearing it now," said Enoch. "It's almost dark."

"Yeah, but they've been wanting to do something besides

stand around and look at it. They've been wanting to help out."

They pulled up the hill and stopped. From between the pickup trucks Mercy came running. Liddle was behind her, and Billy Boy. Then Gyp came steadily in long strides. And there were Gladys and Effie. And Lizzie was coming. Enoch waved to her as he opened the door and got out, bringing the kitten with him. Then he bent down to catch Mercy's arms around his neck. As she hugged him, she saw the kitten, and she pulled back, her eyes wide.

"Oh, Enoch," she said softly, taking it from him, holding it out while it squirmed and kicked, frightened at the gathering crowd.

"Here, you'd better get in the truck with her," said Enoch. "Let her calm down."

"Is it a she?" said Mercy, all her attention on it as she climbed into the truck. "She's so pretty. And she's ours?"

"Sure is," said Enoch. Then he turned back to the others. He let the girls hug him; Gyp clapped him on the shoulder, and so did Billy Boy, reaching up. Then his mother came up, and he gave her a long hug and a kiss and started with her back to the rubble that had been the house. Everyone was there, all the Kettle Creek people and even some long-time locals. They all stopped work and gathered round to greet Enoch, and he moved among them, squeezing hands, patting backs and shoulders, giving hugs. When he came to Rita, he looked squarely at her and smiled and took her offered hands. She seemed different to him, almost like one of the others now. But as he brought back his hands and looked away from her, his eyes slid over her body—still lovely. Then Dee and Dum came out from nowhere and jumped on him, and Bubba, coming up behind the twins, met Enoch's eyes and grinned before his shyness overtook him and made him look away. Enoch touseled his hair and Bubba looked up again, straight into his face, and smiled.

Then everybody went back to work, hurrying against the sunset, filling the pickup trucks with twisted steel roofing and blackened objects of different shapes and sizes. Enoch wandered about, talking to people, looking in the wreckage for things familiar. He came to where Mountain Man was working.

"Can you recognize anything?" said Enoch.

"Some things," said Mountain Man. "Metal stuff mostly." He straightened up and reached around to his back pocket. "Got a present for you," he said, bringing out a pair of worn leather work gloves.

Enoch smiled and took them. "Just what I needed," he said, putting them on.

"That's why I been saving them for you," said Mountain Man. "Now grab ahold of the other end of that sink there, and let's heave her out of here."

For a time Enoch worked beside Mountain Man, throwing things in the truck. Then he stopped and looked around, taking in the valley, the pastures of Wolf Ridge rising behind him, the brown woods of Brokeleg Mountain across the way. He smelled the fresh air and listened to the sounds—no traffic, no sirens, only people talking and cows bawling.

Cows. Enoch suddenly took off his gloves and handed them back to Mountain Man.

"I'm going down to milk," he said.

"Those gloves are yours," said Mountain Man, refusing them. "I ain't never seen you so enthusiastic about milking cows before. You feeling all right?"

"If you only knew how bored I got in Raleigh," said Enoch.

Mountain Man shook his head. "This ain't going to last," he said, chuckling as he turned back to his work. "This ain't going to last a week."

Enoch made his way across the rubble to where Lizzie was working. The sun was low now; they would all be stopping soon.

Lizzie straightened up when she saw him. She smiled, but her face was worn, her eyes sad, and Enoch could see that his homecoming was not enough to wipe away the pain of her loss. It was a fleeting realization, making him feel for an instant grown up and apart. He put his hand on her shoulder.

"I'm sorry about the house," he said.

"I was just thinking," she said. "Yesterday we ate supper right over there." She nodded to where the kitchen used to be. "It was only yesterday. I cooked in my own pots and pans, looked out the window at the sunset, sent Mercy out the back door to get some wood. And tonight there's nothing. Only a pile of ashes and the wide open sky. I don't even own a hairbrush anymore."

"I'll go to town and get you a hairbrush," said Enoch. "But right now I'm going down to milk the cows."

Lizzie laughed softly and hugged him. "I'm glad to have you around again. Just go milk the cows. I can borrow a brush. And come to the Harrimans' when you're through. People have been bringing food all day. We're going to have a fire-and-homecoming party."

"Good," said Enoch. "I need some decent food." He looked around. "Where'd Gyp get to? I want him to go down to the barn with me."

"He's here somewhere," said Lizzie. "Check over on the other side of Stuart's truck."

He went, and for a moment she stood and watched him. Then she turned back to her work.

The barn was unchanged. It was cold, its vastness filled with the smell of hay and manure. Enoch lit the kerosene lamp, and Gyp started up to the loft to throw down some hay. Enoch felt as if he had never been gone, as if the house had never burned, as if he had been here all along, herding the cows to their stalls, drawing milk from their udders, leaning his head against their warm sides, lodging more cow hairs in his red knit cap.

Gyp gave hay to the cows and milked one of them. Then he came and stood at Goldie's stall and watched Enoch. Enoch was glad of his company. He listened as Gyp told him about the fire and about the car Charlie Tate had bought for six hundred dollars and was fixing up. Then Gyp asked him about Raleigh.

"Mostly it was lousy," said Enoch.

"How come?" said Gyp.

"I don't know," said Enoch. "It just was."

"I sort of thought it would be," said Gyp, and Enoch glanced at him and smiled, knowing it was true.

Later, when they were taking the milk to the spring-house, Enoch told him, "I've got a girl back there."

"Then it wasn't that bad," said Gyp.

"Not that part," Enoch replied.

The fire-and-homecoming party was under way when Enoch and Gyp arrived. They filled their plates and went into the living room and sat on the floor by Mercy and Gladys and Mountain Man and Melinda.

Enoch dipped into his chicken pie. "What'd you do with the kitten?" he asked Mercy.

"I put her in Mountain Man's house," said Mercy.

"Y'all are staying with me till Rita leaves," explained Mountain Man.

"You've got room for us all?" said Enoch.

"I got all the room in the world—as long as you don't mind sleeping on the floor."

"It's not that bad," Melinda said to Enoch. "We sent over a mattress for y'all today, and Kate and Morgan chipped in a couple of cots."

"We brought y'all some spare blankets," said Gladys. "So did Brandy."

"I reckon we're in pretty good shape sleepwise," said Mountain Man. "But what about that cat, Miss Mercy? Did you provide her with a place to do her business?"

"I put some dirt in one of your shoes," said Mercy. "Is that all right?"

"You did what?" said Mountain Man, putting down his plate.

Mercy laughed. "I put some dirt in a cardboard box," she said.

"You better have," said Mountain Man.

"So tell us all about Raleigh," Melinda said to Enoch.

"There's not much to tell," said Enoch. "I didn't like it very much."

"Why not?" said Gladys.

"I don't know," said Enoch. "It's hard to say."

"You said a while ago you got bored there," said Mountain Man.

202

"But that's not all of it. There was something missing there. Something we've got here. But I don't know what to say about it. I can't say they should all move to the country. There's not room out here."

"It's not country they're missing anyway," said Mountain Man. "But it's something. They've got to figure out for themselves what it is and how they're going to get it."

"But how are they?" said Enoch.

Mountain Man shook his head. "I don't have the answer."

Enoch scraped up the last of his sweet potatoes. Over by the wood stove Clark was plunking on a guitar, tuning up.

"Where'd you get the guitar, Daddy?" Enoch asked.

"It's Betty's," said Clark.

"Mama's letting him keep it until he gets a new one," said Gladys.

Brandy came in from the kitchen, Dee and Dum and Bubba on her heels. She pulled her fiddle case from beneath the sofa, and the little boys spent a few minutes looking at the fiddle, plinking the strings. Then they came over to Enoch. He set his empty plate away, and Dum dropped into his lap.

"How you doing, Robbie?" said Enoch, squeezing his arm around him.

"Ah, you don't have to call him that," said Mountain Man. "They've given up on it."

"Yeah, I'm Dum," said Dum, bending back his head to look up at Enoch.

"Yeah, he's dumber than a toad frog," said Bubba, sitting himself down on an empty corner of Enoch's lap.

"Toad frogs are smart," said Dum. "You ever seen one catch a bug?"

"There you go, Dum," said Mountain Man. "That's telling him."

"What's come over you, Bubba?" said Enoch. "You're getting mighty bold."

Bubba ducked his face.

"He's going to school," said Gladys.

"I can write my name," said Bubba, looking up.

"Well, I'll be dogged," said Enoch.

"Wonders never cease, do they?" said Mountain Man as he got to his feet.

Over by the wood stove Stuart was tuning his mandolin and Donovan his banjo. Enoch dumped Dum and Bubba off his lap and got up and took his plate to the kitchen. Then he came out and stood by Mountain Man as the band started up with "Old Joe Clark." Mountain Man began to sing, and Enoch did, too, tapping his foot and following Mountain Man's lead for the verses.

I went down to old Joe's house,
Never been there before,
He slept on the feather bed
And I slept on the floor.

More people came around and joined in the singing. Then Mountain Man gave a whoop and started buckdancing. Enoch stepped back with the others to watch him, but Mountain Man motioned for him to join in, and Enoch did, the others clapping and keeping on with their singing, making a circle around the two dancers.

Then Mountain Man fell back, and Enoch was alone, dancing in the center of the circle, feeling good as he looked around at the faces he knew so well, as he felt the music that was so deep in him, that he had known for all his days. He saw Mercy and held out his hand to her, and she came dancing in. Then Mercy held out her hand to Gyp, and Gyp came in. The singing was still going on.

I won't go down to old Joe's house,
I've told you that before,
He fed me in an old hog-trough
And I won't go there no more.

Fare you well, old Joe Clark,
Fare you well, I say,
Fare you well, old Joe Clark,
I ain't got long to stay.

ABOUT THE
AUTHOR

JOYCE ROCKWOOD is the highly acclaimed author of *Long Man's Song*, *To Spoil the Sun*, and *Groundhog's Horse*. She lives with her husband in a small rural community in Georgia.